STAR
YOUNG JEDI KNIGHTS
WARS®

RETURN TO ORD MANTELL

First in an all-new trilogy! A devastating secret from Han's past could spell disaster for the entire Solo family . . .

TROUBLE ON CLOUD CITY

The mysterious Anja Gallandro hatches her sinister plan. A plan that goes far deeper than simple revenge . . .

And don't miss these previous adventures . . .

SHARDS OF ALDERAAN

While visiting the remains of their mother's home planet, Jacen and Jaina encounter a long-lost enemy of the Solo family . . .

DIVERSITY ALLIANCE

Everyone is searching for Bornan Thul, but the young Jedi Knights may be too late—for their true enemy is about to show his shockingly familiar face . . .

DELUSIONS OF GRANDEUR

As the search for Raynar Thul's father continues, the young Jedi Knights turn to a dangerous source for help: the reprogrammed assassin droid, IG-88!

JEDI BOUNTY

Lowbacca has gone to the planet Ryloth to investigate the Diversity Alliance. And the other young Jedi Knights have discovered one truth about the Alliance—you either join, or you die.

THE EMPEROR'S PLAGUE

The young Jedi Knights must destroy the Emperor's Plague before it can be released. But they first must face Nolaa Tarkona—and her very lethal hired hand, Boba Fett.

continued . . .

STAR YOUNG JEDI KNIGHTS *WARS*®

CRISIS AT CRYSTAL REEF

KEVIN J. ANDERSON
and REBECCA MOESTA

BERKLEY JAM BOOKS, NEW YORK

STAR WARS: YOUNG JEDI KNIGHTS:
CRISIS AT CRYSTAL REEF

A Berkley Jam Book / published by arrangement with
Lucasfilm Ltd.

PRINTING HISTORY
Berkley Jam edition / December 1998

The Penguin Putnam Inc. World Wide Web site address is
http://www.penguinputnam.com

Check out the Ace Science Fiction/Fantasy
newsletter, and much more, at Club PPI!

The Official *Star Wars* World Wide Web site address is
http://www.starwars.com

ISBN: 0-425-16519-1

BERKLEY JAM BOOKS®
Berkley Jam Books are published by The Berkley Publishing Group,
a member of Penguin Putnam Inc.,
375 Hudson Street, New York, New York 10014.
BERKLEY JAM and its logo are trademarks
belonging to Berkley Publishing Corporation.

PRINTED IN THE UNITED STATES OF AMERICA

10 9 8 7 6 5 4 3 2 1

This one is for Catherine Ulatowski-Sidor
for helping us look organized even when we're not,
for being there to catch any balls we drop,
for being a careful and enthusiastic reader,
and for being a friend

acknowledgments

Thanks to Matt Bialer and Josh Holbreich of the William Morris Agency for their encouragement on this project; Sue Rostoni, Allan Kausch, and Lucy Autrey Wilson at Lucas Licensing for their valuable input; Ginjer Buchanan and Jessica Faust at Boulevard Books for their unflagging support throughout these fourteen books; Dave Dorman for his fabulous cover art on each and every book; Debra Ray at AnderZone for cheering us on; Sarah Jones at WordFire, Inc., for keeping things running smoothly; and, as always, Jonathan Cowan for being our first test-reader.

A special thanks to the many, many fans who wrote or visited us at book signings to tell us how much the Young Jedi Knights have meant to them. We couldn't have kept going without you.

1

ON THE GRASSY landing field in front of the Jedi academy's Great Temple, an old-model cargo ship gleamed in the morning sun. Though some might have considered the *Lightning Rod* little more than a junk hauler well past its prime—perhaps better suited to be hauled away *as* junk—it was Zekk's pride and joy. The young, dark-haired Jedi walked in a slow circle around his ship, appraising the recent repairs with his sharp emerald gaze.

"You're awfully attached to this scrap heap, aren't you?" Jaina observed with good humor.

Zekk looked into her brandy-brown eyes, raised an eyebrow, and grinned. "Jealous?"

"Maybe just a little." Jaina took a sudden interest in a minute scratch on the hull plating. "Kinda silly, I know. But sometimes I wonder if you don't care about your ship more than, um . . . more than most people do," she finished lamely.

Zekk shrugged. "Why not? Old Peckhum gave me the *Lightning Rod*, and he's the closest thing I've got to a family. This old ship was a special place for us. I practically grew up with her, kind of like you and Jacen did with the *Millennium Falcon*."

Jaina nodded and bit her lower lip. "Sure. I can understand that."

"But there are other reasons that I care more than most people would about this ship," Zekk went on. "Fixing up the *Lightning Rod* was part of my healing process after I left the Shadow Academy." Zekk's face grew serious as he spoke. "And the *Lightning Rod* was with me all through my days as a bounty hunter while we were fighting the Diversity Alliance, while I was learning to trust the Force again."

He gave her a playful look. "Not only that, but it seems like every time I need to fix up my ship, there *you* are helping me." He paused, as if searching for words. "So in a way, you—and Jacen and Lowie and Tenel Ka—are all a part of how I feel about the *Lightning Rod*." Zekk reached out to push a strand of straight brown hair back from Jaina's face.

Her cheeks turned a delicate pink. She opened her mouth as if to answer him.

"Hey, did somebody call us?" Jacen's face appeared over the top of the old light freighter. He waggled his eyebrows comically as Lowie's and Tenel Ka's faces joined his, looking down at Zekk and Jaina.

Tenel Ka's red-gold hair, part of it flowing free

and part fixed in its traditional warrior braids, hung around her face and draped along the *Lightning Rod*'s hull. "We have completed the external hull patch as you requested, Zekk," she announced.

Lowbacca, the lanky young Wookiee, scratched at the dark streak that ran up through his fur above one eye. He rumbled a comment as well. The miniaturized translating droid Em Teedee hovered beside the ginger-furred Wookiee's head. "Oh, indeed, yes! The workmanship is so fine that I daresay it is virtually undetectable—except perhaps by a droid."

Zekk smiled. "Well, thanks everyone, that's great. But I still don't understand why all of you decided the *Lightning Rod* needed an overhaul this morning. It's not as if we're planning a trip."

"Well, no, not exactly . . . ," Jaina said, her voice trailing off. "But there is something—"

"Of course, it never hurts to look your best," Jacen interrupted, jumping down beside his sister and Zekk.

"This is a fact," Tenel Ka said. The warrior girl leapt down to join them.

Lowie looked up at the jungle moon's horizon above the Massassi treetops and gave an inquiring bark. Then, with a joyful bellow, he grabbed the oval translating droid, tucked Em Teedee under one arm, and dove off the side of the *Lightning Rod*. He somersaulted on the short grass and bounded to a standing position beside his friends.

"Well, really, Master Lowbacca!" Em Teedee

scolded as he was being clipped back at his accustomed place on the Wookiee's syren-fiber belt. "Such grandstanding could result in permanent damage to my circuits. Do be careful!"

Zekk ignored the little droid and looked at Lowie. "What did you mean when you said, 'There he is' just before you jumped down here?"

Jaina grinned. "Right on time."

"*Who's* right on time?" Zekk asked in confusion. "Certainly not Anja Gallandro. I haven't seen her all morning."

"Oh," Jacen said, "I forgot to tell you. I checked in on her 'cause she missed morning meal. I asked her to join us, but she said she wasn't feeling well. I believe her. She was shaking all over."

Zekk frowned. "Spice withdrawal?"

Jacen shrugged a shoulder. "That was my guess. Funny thing is, when I asked her why she was shivering, she tried to make it into a joke. Said she'd just been thinking about what the weather must be like on Kessel this time of year."

"Ah. Aha," Tenel Ka said, placing her single hand on her hip. "Definitely spice, then. The spice mines of Kessel are the main source for the drug."

"Anyway, we weren't talking about Anja being on time," Jaina said, getting them back on track. "Look up."

Zekk's face broke into a broad smile as he recognized the enormous modern freighter descending toward the landing field: the *Thunderbolt*.

"It's Peckhum!" he yelled. Zekk ran out onto the flattened grass and began to wave frantically.

"He wanted to surprise you," Jaina said above the whine of the repulsor engines as the ship descended.

"So that's why you wanted the *Lightning Rod* looking her best." Zekk laughed.

"And we got you out onto the landing field without making you suspicious," Jacen added, his brown hair blowing wildly as the *Thunderbolt* approached.

By the time the modern freighter touched down, Zekk was already running toward it, yelling incomprehensible words of greeting. The moment the hatch opened, the old spacer with lanky hair and gray beard stubble started down the ramp. At the same time, Zekk jumped onto the *Thunderbolt*'s still-lowering ramp, bounded up, and met him halfway. Old Peckhum caught him up in a gleeful bear hug as the companions gathered beside the ship to watch.

"So, we surprised him after all, did we?" old Peckhum asked.

"This is a fact," Tenel Ka confirmed.

Peckhum laughed. "I knew I could count on you. Now where's this new young lady you've been talking about in all your messages recently?" he asked, turning to Zekk. "Anja, is it?"

Zekk gave a guilty start, then glanced at Jaina to see if she had noticed. She seemed to be studying something in the grass at her feet. Zekk turned back to the old spacer. "Um, she's not feeling very well. You'll meet her later, Peckhum. But meanwhile, come on into the Jedi academy. I've got a lot to tell you."

•   •   •

Anja Gallandro prowled around the interior of her guest quarters inside the Great Temple. Her agitation would not allow her to sit or stand still for even a moment. Twice already this morning she had ransacked every corner of her room, every pocket of her clothing, every crevice in the cupboards, every fold of her travel bags. It was time she faced the truth.

She had run out of andris spice and there was no more to be found. Still, her huge dark eyes darted around the room searching for inspiration, never resting on any object for more than a second.

Think, she ordered herself. *Think.*

So she thought. But the more Anja thought, the more certain she became that there could be no andris anywhere on Yavin 4, even in the Jedi academy's infirmary.

Anja had insisted to the young Jedi Knights that she was not addicted to spice—that she only used it because she liked the way it made her feel, liked the way it could speed up her reactions and clarify her thoughts. *Andris is an enhancement, not an addiction,* she assured herself.

Then why, she wondered, were her hands trembling? Why was she close to panic at the very thought that she had no way of getting another dose of andris on this tiny backwater moon? And she needed one now.

She growled and shook her head like a nek battle dog on the attack. Her waist-length hair, highlighted by streaks of honey, snapped like a whip made of silky strands.

What was she *doing* on Yavin 4, anyway? It had been her hatred for Han Solo and her belief that he had murdered her father that first motivated her to befriend his twin children, Jacen and Jaina. It had all been part of her plan to take revenge on Solo, either directly or through his children. But now she had gotten to know the twins and their friends and, in spite of the fact that she distrusted and despised their father, she had come to the conclusion that she did not want to hurt them. They didn't deserve it.

Czethros, however, had tried to have them all killed on Cloud City and earlier on the war-torn world of Anobis. Anja no longer trusted her former mentor as she once had.

Still, she wished she could contact him. After all, Czethros had been her main source of spice over the years. He had, in fact, been the first person to show her, years ago, all the benefits andris could provide. He had told her back then that only weaklings became truly addicted. But for the strong-willed, he had insisted, andris was merely a useful tool.

She threaded her shaky fingers through her flowing dark hair and gave it a vicious yank. She had *believed* Czethros. About everything. But Anja was no longer certain what she believed.

With a groan, she threw herself down onto the sleeping pallet and covered her eyes with one arm, trying vainly to slow the rapid beating of her heart. Czethros had lied about the addictiveness of spice.

He had ordered her friends murdered. Perhaps he had lied about Han Solo's role in her father's death as well. . . .

This was the idea she found most difficult to accept. Since childhood, her hatred of Han Solo had given her a focus, someone to blame for everything that had gone wrong in her life. Loathing Solo, and knowing that he was to blame for all her problems, had been one of the few constants she had been able to cling to during the turmoil of her youth.

It would be hard for Anja to give up her hatred—every bit as hard as giving up spice. This was one reason why, in spite of the fact that she now cared about the young Jedi Knights, she still found herself snapping at them, even though they'd done nothing to earn her anger.

Unable to stay still any longer, Anja pushed herself up off the sleeping pallet and began prowling her chambers again.

"I've got it under control," she gritted through clenched teeth. "I can handle this." She reached behind her head and retied the leather band she wore around her forehead to keep her flowing hair in check. Although she hadn't been doing any real physical activity, perspiration dripped from under the headband and down the back of her neck.

"*I can handle this*," she repeated, more forcefully.

But Anja knew she was lying to herself.

2

ALONE IN A workroom by an outer wall of the Great Temple, Zekk sat next to the table and listened to the rainstorm outside. Old Peckhum had gone to see Master Skywalker, and Zekk was spending some time by himself, working hard. He could smell the spattering droplets of fresh water that moistened the chiseled stone of the rebuilt pyramid's walls.

Open window slits allowed the calming noises of the afternoon rain shower to drift in along with the wonderful jungle scents, without letting the water leak into the rooms. The huge orange planet Yavin had set behind the Jedi academy, leaving only dim and distant sunlight to penetrate the storm clouds. In the sky above the thick treetops, a fresh crop of kite plants blossomed in brilliant colors, drifting about on the winds and soaking up the falling rain.

Peace . . . calm . . . thoughts of the light side of the Force.

After he had recentered his concentration, Zekk turned back to constructing his new lightsaber. Tools lay strewn about on the stone table surface, and bright light spilled down from a single glow-panel to illuminate his efforts.

He had moved to this study room from his own quarters so he could be alone, so he could think. Zekk needed to focus on the important task at hand. Building a personal lightsaber was an assignment reserved for trained and trusted Jedi Knights—and he intended to do his best work. This time.

As he picked up the components, aligned them, tightened connectors, adjusted the power pack, he felt a turmoil in his heart. He had wielded a lightsaber many times in the service of the Shadow Academy. But back then, when the dark Jedi Brakiss had taught him how to use the energy blade, Zekk had never gone through this rite of passage.

The Shadow Academy had manufactured cheap and identical lightsabers by the dozen, presenting them to their evil-trained students during practice sessions and before the attack on the New Republic. Zekk had had a lightsaber *given* to him—but he hadn't ever built his own.

Zekk had never felt such an attachment to any weapon before. At the Shadow Academy, the light-saber with which he had dueled and led the attack on Yavin 4 was simply a *tool*, interchangeable with anyone else's. This energy blade, though, would be his *own*. Zekk would never make the mistake of falling to the dark side again. He understood that everything about this weapon was his responsibility. Building a lightsaber was so . . . personal.

When he had attempted the delicate task back in his own quarters, though, an anxious Jaina had hovered behind him, looking over his shoulder, making suggestions, and tinkering with the components. Then Jacen had arrived, spouting conversation and the usual string of jokes. Lowie had leaned in, groaning and growling in the Wookiee language, to ask if Zekk needed any assistance. His friends all meant well, but what he needed most was *to be alone* . . . to do this himself.

Peckhum's recent arrival had reminded Zekk of his youth on Coruscant, simpler times when Jacen and Jaina and Zekk had been carefree friends . . . back before he had betrayed them. Zekk had learned to overcome the guilt from the bad things he had done, but he'd never forgotten. What mattered most was who he was *now* and who he would become in the future.

Outside, flying creatures swooped high in the air with jaws wide open. They snatched the colorful kite plants from the sky and dragged them down to the treetops to feed, all the while scattering jewel-like spores that helped the drifting life-forms reproduce.

Zekk fitted the last components together, then took the lightsaber apart again, triple-checking the connections and alignments before he snapped the casing closed for the last time. He held the new weapon in his hand, squeezed the polished grip, examined the power studs, flicked the hilt from side to side to test its weight and balance. Somehow he was reluctant to switch on the lightsaber, afraid that he might have done something wrong.

"Do, or do not. There is no try," Zekk muttered to himself.

He pressed the power stud—and the lightsaber flared to life at the first touch. The throbbing blade glowed a pure yellow-orange, like a captured flame enclosed in a long, thin tube. With the greatest care, he moved his weapon, and the ionization thrum made a musical sound in the air. The lightsaber felt *right* in his hand—not a seductive power that he might be tempted to misuse, but a precise and well-controlled weapon that fit him perfectly. A Jedi weapon . . . for a Jedi Knight.

Relief washed through him. Zekk allowed himself a contented smile. He held the flame-orange blade high. The bright glow on his face seemed like a purifying fire. He had come through his long ordeal and survived. From now on, everything would be right.

Nothing would ever be right again.

Anja tossed and turned in her room and finally rolled over to slam her fist against the hard stone wall. The pain jarred her thoughts, distracted her for just an instant. But the stinging of her knuckles rapidly faded to a dull throb, far overshadowed by the demanding outcry of need that coursed through her body. *Andris . . . andris . . . andris . . .*

Anja had thought she could stand it for as long as necessary, but time had only amplified the pain until the screaming need inside her head became unbearable. She couldn't kid herself any longer. Czethros had gone into hiding after the disaster on Cloud City. He would never provide her with the supply of spice she desperately needed. Anja couldn't count on him, and she couldn't survive if she didn't get another dose of andris—and soon.

She would have to get some herself. She would go right to the source. There was no other way. She had to take matters into her own hands.

Anja certainly couldn't obtain any spice here on Yavin 4, definitely not at the Jedi academy. These students of the Force seemed to draw their pleasure simply from staring at rocks and meditating. She had tried, but that just didn't work for her. Anja had always been independent. When a problem presented itself, she faced the challenge, she devised a solution, she found a way.

She got up from her sweat-soaked bed, turned the glowpanel to its lowest setting, and dressed quietly. The rain had stopped late that afternoon, and the Great Temple had fallen into a peaceful quietness as the other Jedi students slept or practiced their mind-intensive studies. Anja gathered her few meager supplies, hesitated before she clipped her antique lightsaber in place on her belt. Without the boost she received from a dose of spice, she didn't know how well she could use the Jedi weapon.

Anja again retied her leather headband around

her forehead to hold back her long, streaked hair. She tucked her boots under her arms and scurried barefoot across the cold stone floor.

She froze in the shadows as she heard the rolling hum and saw the blinking form of Artoo-Detoo trundling down one of the corridors ahead. Fortunately, the little astromech droid turned left and disappeared into the shadows without seeing her. She drew in a deep breath and started moving again.

Anja hurried until she reached the opening down to the hangar beneath the pyramid. Standing in the cool shadows, she looked around, trying to make her choice from the ships parked there. She knew she could fly any craft. She'd been trained for years as a smuggler, flying from Ord Mantell back to her war-torn homeworld of Anobis. She needed something fast, without markings.

The *Lightning Rod*.

Ducking low, Anja crept to the door of the hangar bay and looked across the landing field toward Zekk's battered craft. Old man Peckhum, who had used the stock light freighter for many years to haul supplies in and around the New Republic, had given it to Zekk as his personal ship.

Anja had no choice. She had to get away, to get what she needed before the pain overwhelmed her. Anja's eyes narrowed, and she allowed herself to focus on nothing beyond her goal. Her feet made no noise on the dew-soaked grass as she ran across the landing field to the *Lightning Rod* and up the still-open ramp. She slipped into the worn cockpit seat, strapped herself down, and powered up the engines.

Security was lax here on Yavin 4. With so many Jedi Knights around, Luke Skywalker seemed to believe they could drive back any military assault; a New Republic fleet in orbit also helped to protect the academy. But no one would stop her from the inside. She could take the little freighter, fly out, and dive into hyperspace before anyone reacted quickly enough to question her.

When she powered up the repulsorjets, a sleepy guard came running to the distant door of the hangar bay and stared in surprise at the commandeered ship. He waved, signaling for her to wait, but Anja punched the engines, raised the craft off the field, and streaked out over the treetops.

The *Lightning Rod* rapidly left the tall Massassi pyramid behind, flying low over the jungle canopy to foil any scanning attempts. The tangled foliage was like a lumpy carpet below her. After she had rounded the sharp curve of the small moon, Anja arced off into space.

Determined to let nothing distract her from her goal, Anja ignored the comm chatter as alarms were raised. She would be gone well before the defensive fleet could intercept her.

Anja set the coordinates in the *Lightning Rod*'s navicomputer, filling them in from memory. Spice . . . she had to have spice. There was no time to weigh the many options: she would go directly to the source.

Starlines unfolded around her and the *Lightning Rod* plunged into hyperspace . . . heading for Kessel.

3

IT WAS THE start of as perfect a morning as Zekk could ever remember. Outside, bright sunshine poured down on the Jedi academy, and a fresh breeze carrying the scents of a thousand luscious jungle plants wafted in through the thick stone window openings. The young Jedi Knights were used to getting up very early, and today they had special reason, since Peckhum was due to leave.

At morning meal, Jaina greeted Zekk and Peckhum with a hug. There had been no mistaking the pride in her eyes when she saw the new lightsaber hanging at Zekk's belt. "Looks like a fine weapon, Zekk. If you want a sparring partner later on, come see me."

"After I show Master Skywalker."

"Hey," Jacen said as he sauntered in, grinning. "Two Gamorrean guards are walking down a narrow, deserted canyon when suddenly a rancor comes out and starts chasing them. One of the Gamorreans stops to put on his best running shoes. 'Don't waste time,' shouts the other one, 'you can't outrun a rancor with those!' 'I don't have to outrun a rancor,' says the first one as he finishes lacing his shoes, 'I just have to outrun *you*!'" A chorus of chuckles and groans rewarded him.

With additional jokes, Jacen was in rare form during the meal, and they all laughed so hard it was difficult not to choke as they ate. Tenel Ka offered a rare toast of friendship to the entire group seated at their table. Lowie surprised them all by presenting a dramatic Wookiee speech while Em Teedee provided hilariously inaccurate translations, which the companions now recognized with their increasing grasp of Lowbacca's native language.

Jaina, sparkling with good humor, teased old Peckhum throughout the meal and squeezed Zekk's hand under the table. The old spacer laughed and enjoyed the attention.

Even when it was time for Peckhum to go, Zekk's mood could not be dampened. "I'm sorry you couldn't meet Anja," he told the spacer. "I knocked on the door to her quarters, but she didn't answer. Must be keeping to herself again. She's got . . . a lot of things to work out in her head. Besides, her communication skills aren't always the greatest."

As they left the temple and walked through the dim corridors leading out, old Peckhum gave Zekk a mock stern look. "Speaking of, uh, communication skills—if I hadn't switched schedules with another freighter pilot so that I could come to Yavin 4 and visit my favorite Jedi trainee, I might not've heard about your progress for another month. You didn't mention you were going to build a lightsaber last week when I talked to you."

Zekk hunched his shoulders. "I'm sorry I didn't tell you. I guess maybe I was afraid I'd fail. There was always a chance that I might build a faulty weapon and I'd have to throw it away and start all over. Worse, I thought maybe the wrong kind of blade might try to draw me back toward the dark side."

The old spacer gave a thoughtful nod. "I understand that, but don't forget that you can trust me. I'd like to know whenever something important is going on in your life. I'm always willing to rearrange my schedule so I can share a special occasion with you."

Jaina snorted. "And you can put that nonsense about going over to the dark side behind you, Zekk."

"Thanks for trusting me," Zekk said in a low voice as they all emerged into the sunlight in front of the Jedi academy. "That trust was what gave me the strength to leave the dark side for good."

"The trust of friends is rare and important," Tenel Ka observed. Lowie crooned his agreement.

They walked down the temple steps toward the landing field. Several New Republic soldiers milled about taking readings at a freshly scorched spot on the ground. A group of assorted investigators stood inside the small craft bay on the pyramid's lowest level, talking in urgent tones with the night-shift guard who had been on duty the evening before.

Preoccupied with the old man's departure, the companions began walking across the grass with Peckhum toward the *Thunderbolt*. Suddenly, Zekk stopped and turned back to the burned, empty spot on the landing field. His mouth fell open. He blinked in confusion. "You didn't have to move my ship inside, Jaina. I would have done it myself. Of course, I know that flying a ship is never hard work for you, but—"

"No," Jaina said. "I haven't been anywhere near the *Lightning Rod* this morning."

"Something's wrong," Jacen said.

Old Peckhum looked curiously at the spot where his former ship had been when he arrived the day before. But the *Lightning Rod* was nowhere to be seen.

"Ah," Tenel Ka said in a matter-of-fact voice. "Aha."

Jacen drew a deep breath, let it out slowly. "I've got a *bad* feeling about this."

Inside the shadows of the small craft bay, Luke Skywalker left the other members of the investigative team and marched purposefully toward Zekk. The dark-haired young man felt a cold twist in his stomach as his suspicions grew. Master Skywalker looked directly into his green eyes.

"Zekk, I'm afraid Anja has taken your ship."

• • •

Later, after Peckhum's tight schedule had forced him to leave, the young Jedi gathered in Luke Skywalker's office. Jaina squirmed as she watched a storm of emotions cross Zekk's face. "Anja *stole* the *Lightning Rod*!" he said through gritted teeth. "She ran away from the Jedi academy."

Luke nodded patiently. "She caught the hangar guard by surprise and took off before any of the orbital forces could stop her."

Zekk went on, fuming. "Anja is a thief, and I want my ship back. What are we going to do about it? We've got to find her."

Jaina cleared her throat. "We could, um, ask Mom and Dad to send out some security forces. Maybe they can track down the *Lightning Rod*, wherever Anja's taken it?"

"Or they could probably issue some bulletins to the authorities on various planets. . . ." Jacen's voice trailed off.

Luke raised his eyebrows and pursed his lips, waiting for a full minute of silence before he spoke. "As for Anja leaving the Jedi academy, that is her choice. Not only is she an adult, she's not exactly a Jedi. We can't stop her from leaving if she wants to."

"But she can't take my ship to do it," Zekk said.

"No. That's true enough. But first—" he spread his hands and gazed around at his assembled students "—you tell me. Is she a criminal or a friend? Would you like to have her arrested?"

Zekk squirmed at the Jedi Master's question. "Too bad we can't still send people to the spice mines of Kessel," he grumbled.

Each of the young Jedi shook their heads in turn.

"Incarceration would serve no purpose," Tenel Ka said. "I believe she must have been desperate."

Jaina looked down at her hands in her lap. "And I think we all know *why* she was desperate."

Lowie woofed an observation. Jacen nodded and in a low voice said, "Spice."

"She was going through withdrawal," Zekk said, meeting Master Skywalker's eyes.

"Do you believe she intends to keep your ship— or even sell it?" Luke asked. "In order to get credits to buy spice?"

Jaina was surprised when they all reacted instantly. Lowie bellowed a protest. "Indeed not!" Em Teedee added.

"She wouldn't do that. I think she's planning to bring it back," Jacen said in a confident voice.

Jaina bit her lower lip. "I have a feeling she's in more trouble than we know."

Luke stood. "Then I'd say this isn't exactly a job for New Republic security. Don't you think this is a situation that her friends, five Jedi Knights—not to mention one extremely talented droid—could handle on their own?"

They all agreed, and the Jedi Master left them alone to discuss the details.

"At least we've got the *Rock Dragon*," Jaina said. "She's a good fast ship."

"But how do we find her? We can hardly go running from system to system with a large holograph asking, 'Have you seen this girl?'" Jacen pointed out.

Lowie gave a long grumble. "Master Lowbacca suggests that perhaps we could consult with some of the guardian forces stationed in orbit around this moon."

"They might have tracked the *Lightning Rod*'s initial vector," Jaina agreed.

Zekk shrugged. "I'll take any lead we can get."

Within five minutes the companions all stood in the comm center. On half of the screen, a weary-eyed officer who was obviously off-duty rubbed a hand over his eyes. The other half of the screen displayed a starmap.

"I'm sorry," the shift officer said, "we tried to scan the ship's navicomputer before it went into hyperspace, but the most we were able to determine was that the *Lightning Rod* was heading for one of the systems in this sector. It still covers hundreds of planets, though." Glowing white lines appeared around a segment of space in the starmap. "I've got a team on it."

"Hey, thanks," Jacen said, trying to sound enthusiastic. "You've been a big help." The portion of the screen that held the officer's face went blank, leaving only the starmap.

Tenel Ka's cool gray eyes narrowed suddenly, as if something important had just occurred to her. "Jacen, my friend, what joke did Anja attempt to make yesterday when you sensed she was going through withdrawal?"

He shrugged. "I can't remember her exact words. Something about Kessel, but I don't see what that has to do—*oh*!"

Jaina said, "Under stress, it's not unusual for people to joke about what's really on their minds."

"Zekk also mentioned the spice mines," Tenel Ka pointed out. "Perhaps because of Anja's addiction, or because of her joke."

A slow grin spread across Zekk's face. He pointed toward the starmap still covering half the screen. "And Kessel just happens to be right in the middle of that sector."

4

AFTER YEARS OF running the spice mines of Kessel, Chief Administrator Nien Nunb finally thought that the place felt like the warrens of home. The dim winding tunnels with their cool rock walls seemed much like the crowded burrows that honeycombed the crust of Sullust, where mousy-faced, large-eyed Sullustan families preferred to live together. Nien Nunb often went back home to visit his family, whenever he could spare himself here.

The spice mines had once been a feared place, an Imperial prison planet and work camp. But over a decade ago Lando Calrissian had purchased the mines, setting up his friend and copilot Nien Nunb as their administrator. Together, they had turned the once-dreaded mines into a productive industrial facility that held few of the grim connotations that Kessel formerly had. They'd found a way to turn it into a true credit-making enterprise.

By choosing alien species who were *comfortable* underground, who *preferred* living in tunnels and in darkness, Nien Nunb had made the place an efficient working environment. Spice production had increased greatly in the past ten years. Nien Nunb and his old friend Lando liked to joke that the mines were one of Calrissian's few ventures that actually turned a profit, although the initial investment for extensive revamping and new equipment had cost an emperor's ransom.

In his younger years, Nien Nunb had led a life of adventure, tagging along with Lando on smuggling runs, breaking through Imperial blockades and delivering much-needed supplies to restricted planets. In the *Millennium Falcon*, borrowed from Han Solo, Nien Nunb had served as copilot when Lando made his desperate run to destroy the second Death Star. Nervous by nature, Nien Nunb had been certain they would die in the attempt . . . but somehow the *Falcon* had survived, and Lando had gone on to become a hero of the New Republic.

But the Sullustan copilot had had enough excitement in his life, and now he was content just to work here in the calming twisted tunnels beneath the cold surface of Kessel. He liked running a business. He thought it much better than getting shot at every other day.

Kessel was a small, low-gravity world, roughly potato-shaped, with a very thin atmosphere. Like Sullust, the planet was habitable only belowground, behind the sealed entrances to the dark tunnels.

Large cities and giant atmospheric generation plants had been established to stabilize the amount of air clinging to the surface, but Kessel's gravity was simply not strong enough to keep all of the atmosphere from escaping into space.

Whenever he looked through the panoramic viewing ports up into the sky, the Chief Administrator could see a ring of broken meteors strewn out about the planet, shards from Kessel's companion moon. They orbited, glittering with reflected light, and even during dim daylight, a sparkling show of meteors rained down to pound the surface of the mining planet. Fortunately, no one lived out there in the hazardous zone.

The Death Star prototype had destroyed Kessel's moon during the resurgence of Imperial activity many years before. Since that time, though, Kessel had been a quiet place, as if the whole planet had decided to take a deep breath and regather its energy.

Because of the spice's desirable effects—a burst of energy or telepathic enhancement—many black-market entrepreneurs sold spice illicitly. Spies, smugglers, and information brokers used it, as did thrill seekers. As a result, the substance became rare and too little was left for the legitimate users throughout the New Republic. Spice was vital for many medical treatments: to save weakened patients, to restore the memories of amnesia victims, to enhance communication in deeply impaired individuals, and so on.

Because of the long and well-established tradition of illegal spice distribution, Nien Nunb had taken years to crack down on the edge-of-the-law traders. His kindheartedness had paid off. Happy workers had rewarded the Chief Administrator by finding a rich new strike of andris spice on the far side of Kessel. Nien Nunb was exceedingly pleased.

Andris, a rare form of the drug, was as valuable as glitterstim or ryll. Its properties were further enhanced by exposure to extreme cold. Much andris had already been excavated here on Kessel, bringing excellent financial returns on the new mine. Seeing the opportunity to increase the potency of the andris (and their profits as well), Nien Nunb and his workers had recently completed installing a carbon-freezing facility in the main processing center.

Today was just another day at work, as the Sullustan accompanied his Second Administrator, Torvon, on their weekly inspection tour. Together, the tall administrator and the short, mousy manager entered a main work chamber.

In the enormous hollowed-out room below the surface, holding pits and carbonite generators bubbled and steamed under a rocky ceiling. Cold white mist oozed out of exhaust valves on a rattling conveyor. Blind beetlelike creatures worked with multiple claws, packaging and sealing the purified andris before it was sent into the hissing vat of pure carbonite that had been freshly delivered from the rings of the Empress Teta system.

Torvon's high shiny forehead was split into hemispheres that implied an increased cranial capacity. The tall secondary administrator had solid pale green eyes with no pupils Nien Nunb could see. Torvon had come highly recommended after serving as a high-ranking administrator in no less than six other financially successful industrial facilities. The man was so tall that the Sullustan's shoulders barely came up to his knobby knees.

As he walked beside his secondary administrator, Nien Nunb studied the details with his huge black eyes, which glinted as he flicked his gaze along the assembly line. The blind beetles seemed perfectly happy with their work. They were well fed, well paid, and lived in a community in abandoned glitterstim tunnels on the far side of Kessel. They asked for little else.

Lift platforms carried sealed, code-numbered crates of processed andris up to the surface, where a domed spaceport received the cargo for shipping. Armed vessels flew off to deliver the treasure. Each cargo ship received a percentage, and the remaining credits were transmitted back to Kessel.

Ventilation ducts and piping thrummed around the generators and cold-storage receptacles. Machinery protruded above and below, fitting together in a jigsaw puzzle of controlled chaos that offered a variety of small crannies and hollows to be used for equipment storage. Nien Nunb noted ways to make more efficient use of space. Perhaps employees from other areas could bring their storage items in here.

He studied the monitor panels and controls as the brooding Torvon stepped close beside him, towering like a tree. The Sullustan manager glanced at the pressure gauges of flowing raw carbonite and noticed that many of the needles had edged up into the red zones. He muttered in alarm and tapped one of the dials, double-checking the reading. Torvon reached up out of sight and fiddled with one of the controls. Nien Nunb assumed he had seen the same problem and was working to correct it.

Suddenly the gauges jumped. The readings went much higher—much too fast. What had Torvon done?

Nien Nunb gave a loud squawk of alarm. He heard a faint creaking groan, saw that one of the coolant pipes close to him was bulging, buckling with the strain. He cried out and instinctively dove headfirst into a protected cranny between two huge pieces of equipment.

Torvon's knobby legs appeared, striding closer to where Nien Nunb had taken shelter. The Sullustan yelled for the secondary administrator to get out of the way, but instead Torvon bent over, his unreadable pale green eyes flashing. He reached into the cranny, trying to grab Nien Nunb. *Couldn't Torvon see the danger? What was he doing?* The Sullustan couldn't understand why he didn't get out of the way. A moment later, Torvon's hands clutched Nien Nunb's vest and began to drag him out.

Torvon was going to haul him *into* the line of the accident!

Just then, though, the groaning pipe burst. *Too soon.*

Gushing, infinitely cold vapors blasted Torvon's legs, right where he'd been trying to pull Nien Nunb. The carbonite instantly froze the tall administrator's joints, turning his lower legs into poles of solid ice. Torvon howled in shock and tried to move out of the way, but his feet were stuck to the floor. The tall man bent over, tugging at his feet, but his legs, like sticks of brittle kindling, shattered. Torvon fell face-first into the blast of ultrafrigid gas.

The carbonite did its work, even as the murderous administrator's broken body fell, freezing his head and body core absolutely solid in the fraction of a second it took for him to tumble the remaining distance to the hard stone floor. When he struck the unyielding surface, Torvon smashed into a million glittering pieces. His hand still clutched Nien Nunb's vest—not frozen, but no longer alive.

The Sullustan manager backed up to huddle in the cranny again, terrified but unhurt.

Alarms sounded. Lights flashed. Automatic systems sealed off the breached carbonite tube, preventing further loss of the precious freezing substance.

Within moments the air would clear, though Nien Nunb didn't know if he would ever be able to drive

away the chill in his heart. He had trusted Torvon—
and Torvon had tried to kill him. Hadn't he? Nien
Nunb shook his head to clear it. He didn't know
what exactly had gone on here, and he doubted
anyone else would give him the answers—but the
Chief Administrator knew for certain that this was
no mere accident.

Torvon had died, but the actual target must have
been Nien Nunb himself.

5

WHEN ANJA HEADED for Kessel in the stolen *Lightning Rod*, it felt just like old times. She was flying in a ship as an independent pilot—just like the smuggler and expediter she had been for Czethros. She could take care of herself. She always had. Anja had her wits about her, and she had the antique lightsaber she had bought from a scavenger merchant in an illicit market on Ord Mantell. She didn't need the Solo twins or their friends to solve her problems for her.

She could handle this.

As she came in to the Kessel system, she steered clear of the treacherous conglomeration of black holes known as the Maw Cluster, which had given rise to the classic challenge of the "Kessel Run." Kessel itself, a small world not much bigger than a planetoid, was surrounded by a wispy white mane of atmosphere that leaked away into space like a comet's tail.

The shattered moon, blasted apart by the proto-type Death Star, had turned into countless obstacles in the sky, but Anja was confident in her piloting abilities. She locked onto the spaceport beacon, and the *Lightning Rod* cruised down through the atmosphere, banging and bouncing as it struck meteors too tiny to be marked on any hazard charts.

"Spaceport Control, this is an unlicensed trader," she said into the comm system. "I wish to land for maintenance and services. I'm out of Ord Mantell and ran into some damage flying too close to the black holes out there."

"You're far from home, unlicensed trader," said the attendant.

"Yeah, right. And I'm trying to get back there," Anja replied. "Do you have a maintenance dock I could hire?"

"Follow this vector," came the answer. Coordinates scrolled up on her screen. Anja smiled, followed the beacon to a contained cargo area at those coordinates, and approached the opening dome to land.

Anja felt the hunger screaming inside her more stridently than ever. Down beneath the white alkaline surface of Kessel, hidden in the rocks of this planet, was *spice* . . . spice for the taking. All she needed for now was one more dose just to help her get by. She only had to track down a sample, just a tiny amount. That would buy her more time in which to battle her addiction.

She hadn't been lying to Jacen and Jaina Solo

when she'd said she only took andris because she liked to. Just for kicks. She had believed that. Sometimes she did need spice, though. And the twins had made her realize, reluctantly, that she needed andris more than she had let herself believe.

Anja Gallandro did not like to depend on anyone or anything. She *had* to kick this habit, break her addiction . . . and she would start as soon as she formed a plan. After she got herself another dose to tide her over, she would be able to think more clearly.

But now that she was on Kessel, with the *Lightning Rod* settled into an unmarked berth inside the enclosed cargo bay, she didn't know how to go about obtaining a new supply. Security would be tight. Although smugglers sometimes made a living from selling andris and glitterstim and ryll offworld, she couldn't just step into the local mercantile and order a container for herself.

But she hoped there might be some people in the docking bays who had a tiny bit of skim they could sell from their cargo . . . under the table, of course.

She stepped out of the cooling *Lightning Rod*, looked around, and tossed her long hair behind her back. She still wore her skintight outfit from her smuggling days. The sleeveless shirt showed off her taut muscles and the piranha beetle tattoo on her arm. But Kessel was a cold world, and even here in the docking bay she felt a bite to the air. Shivering, she considered going back into the *Lightning Rod* to rummage through the supply compartments and find warmer clothes.

But then her eyes fixed on a familiar craft at the other side of the docking bay. She was puzzled for a moment. She'd seen the ship not long before. When a little grayish-skinned man with winglike eyebrows and a ridged scalp emerged, she put the pieces together instantly. She remembered this man and his ship.

Lilmit.

His craft was the *Rude Awakening*, a cargo hauler licensed out of Ord Mantell. Lilmit had been on his way from Ord Mantell to Anja's homeworld of Anobis, hauling a load of black-market weapons. Those contraband tools of destruction were for sale to one of the sides fighting in the ongoing civil war that had devastated Anobis for decades. Worst of all, Lilmit was no mere gunrunner: he was an opportunist without a conscience. He had sold weapons to *both* sides in the conflict, making his profit by perpetuating the destruction, the misery, the bloodshed.

Han Solo had stopped Lilmit's ship, using the *Millennium Falcon* to intimidate him. Together, Anja and the young Jedi Knights had boarded the *Rude Awakening*, discovered the weapons cache, and destroyed all the deadly items in an explosion in space. It was one of the few good things Han Solo had ever done, as far as Anja was concerned.

And now she had caught Lilmit here on Kessel, no doubt causing more problems.

Before she could stop herself, Anja sprinted across the enclosed cargo bay, her long legs carrying her rapidly in the low gravity. Lilmit looked up from tinkering in his open engine compartments. He saw her coming and either recognized her or instinctively drew back from the blazing fire in her large eyes. He raised his webbed hands and backed against the hull of his ship in surrender.

Anja was there, glaring down at him. "What are you doing here, little man? Procuring more weapons?"

"No, no!" the diminutive smuggler said, flapping his fingers. "There's nothing in my cargo that would interest you. It has nothing to do with you—and Czethros would be very angry if you sabotaged me again."

Czethros? Anja drew back. "What are you talking about?"

Lilmit misinterpreted her question. "Don't think I've forgotten you. Your name is Anja Gallandro, and I found out that you work for Czethros, too. You were with Han Solo, and you helped him destroy my entire cargo on its way to Anobis. Czethros really didn't seem surprised when I told him. Oh, he was displeased to hear that you cost him most of his business on Anobis, but he was most displeased with me. He said your assignment was your business, and my assignment was *my* responsibility. *I* had to pay Czethros back for that loss out of my personal accounts. I barely kept my family from being sold into slavery. Now that I'm almost back on my feet, I won't let you destroy my work again. I can't afford it."

"Czethros . . . you're *sure* you work for him?" Anja said, thinking of how Czethros had pretended to be her friend, taken her under his wing, trained her on Ord Mantell. How could he be involved in such terrible things? Of course, he *had* ordered his henchmen to kill the young Jedi Knights. . . .

"Yes!" Lilmit insisted. "Just as you do! But after that disaster of losing all the weapons, Czethros assigned somebody else to those duties and transferred me to the spice run instead. *Please*—don't ruin this for me." His voice carried a whining tone.

"I wouldn't do that to you," she said masking her confusion with a smooth reply. "We're colleagues, right?" She fell silent, hoping he would blunder through more of an explanation. But already Lilmit's words echoed like thunder through her head. Czethros himself had been involved in the gun-running to Anobis!

She couldn't believe it. He had *lied* to her! And not just about the addictive properties of spice. He'd known all along how much she despised the endless conflict on her war-torn world. He had pretended to understand what Anja had been through. Czethros had consoled her, offered her a new chance at life, given her a job working for him. And all the while he had secretly been selling weapons so that the people on her world could destroy themselves!

He was a liar *and* a traitor.

Czethros had played her for a fool. He'd kept his true activities secret. He'd used her. In fact, Anja suddenly found it easy to accept that, in all likelihood, the man had purposely addicted her to spice just to keep her under his thumb.

It made complete sense now. Czethros was not a generous or benevolent man. He had managed to trap Anja in a prison of her own anger and need, and now that she *needed* the andris more than anything else . . . he had run. He'd disappeared, gone into hiding to protect his own skin. He didn't care about her at all.

Her face hardened into a grim scowl. "And just where were you intending to go, Lilmit? You have a shipment of spice, you say?"

"I'm picking one up today. Just a small shipment," the smuggler said. "Taking it to Mon Calamari. Czethros probably told you all about the Black Sun activities there. We've been building up quite a spice stash close to Crystal Reef, their largest resort city, near the Arctic. We hide the andris in the water beneath the polar ice caps to keep it potent. From there, we plan to sell it to select clientele in the floating casinos. The profits from this operation alone could make Czethros a wealthy man for the rest of his life. There's a thriving black market. Only the wealthiest people from all over the New Republic can afford to stay on one of those oceangoing resorts. Especially Crystal Reef."

Anja nodded slowly. A stash of andris on the ocean world. . . . Black Sun agents making illicit drug sales to customers in the floating casinos. It all made sense now. Czethros was indeed part of Black Sun, perhaps one of its leaders. He already had his claws into the gambling and entertainment on Cloud City. He stockpiled drugs on Mon Calamari . . . and had been running weapons to the civil war on Anobis, all the while pretending to be her friend and protector. Many of Anja's people had died because of him. She began to wonder how many pots Czethros was stirring that she didn't know about yet.

"Tell me the coordinates of your stash, Lilmit," she said. "How do I find it? I'll be taking over this run from you."

Lilmit blanched. "No, please!"

"It's all right. I've been testing you," she said. "For Czethros. He wanted to be sure you were up to the new assignment." She paused, thinking fast. "You'll make the delivery to Coruscant. I'll take care of Mon Calamari, because—because it falls into my new territory. I'm surprised Czethros didn't warn you."

Lilmit said, "But what you ask is impossible. I couldn't possibly make it past security to Coruscant with a load of spice."

She sighed and shook her head in a disgusted fashion. "I told him he wouldn't be able to entrust this mission to you, but he assured me you wouldn't disappoint him again. . . ."

"Wait! No. I can do this. If Czethros is trusting me to pull this mission off, then I will."

"Good. Now tell me how to find the stash of andris on Mon Calamari. Czethros has ordered me to move it."

In a stuttering voice, Lilmit told her. He gave her

maps and the transponder frequency of the stash so that she could locate the supply in the extremely cold waters of the ocean world's polar seas.

"I need to hurry," Lilmit said, his voice quavering. "I don't have much cargo, but . . ." He looked around furtively, anxiously. The other people in the domed space dock didn't seem to feel his nervousness. "*You* know something's about to happen here—and it's got to be very soon now. Czethros has plans for Kessel." He lowered his voice. "Between you and me, I don't want to be here when his troops come in for the big takeover."

"When?" Anja said.

"*I* don't know. If he didn't tell you, he certainly wouldn't have told *me*." Lilmit shrugged. "But these people don't suspect at all, and I don't want to be here during all the blaster fire. I need to get off this planet."

"You will," Anja said. "But I'm leaving first."

"Wait. Why didn't Czethros tell me about this change of plans?" Lilmit wanted to know.

"You said yourself there are many things Czethros tells me that he wouldn't tell you," Anja said.

"All right." Lilmit glanced furtively around. "Just don't let Czethros touch my family."

Remembering that Lilmit had a family—one that he had barely kept out of slavery—Anja felt a pang of conscience. Although this man had smuggled who knows how many weapons to Anobis to fuel the war there, Anja found it harder to judge him now. She herself could no longer justify all of the work that she had done in Czethros's service. She couldn't even be certain that she *knew* the consequences of all of the tasks she had performed for him.

"If all goes according to plan, I assure you Czethros will *never* touch or threaten your family again," she said.

Lilmit's eyes lit with enthusiasm and wonder. "Then this assignment *is* important."

Anja cocked her head to one side and gave him a wordless look that said, *Of course. What did I tell you?*

"Now, I'm going to need two doses of spice before I head out," Anja said briskly, folding her arms across her chest and fixing him with a no-nonsense stare. She cast about in her mind for a good reason. "Uh, Czethros has asked me to do a bit of . . . *spying* for him while I'm on Mon Calamari." She gave a meaningful lift to her eyebrows.

"Oh, I see. Certainly," Lilmit said, hurrying into his ship and returning moments later with two insulated cryovials and a miniature carbon-freeze unit. "He told me I might need to be flexible on this assignment. Now I understand." He handed her the vials. "Czethros warned me I wouldn't be able to contact him until everything was 'in place.' So when you speak to him next time, tell him that I got the message. I won't let anything get in my way this time, not even Han Solo himself."

Anja tucked the two insulated vials into a pocket, then graced him with a thin smile. "I see Czethros was right about you after all, Lilmit. I'll remember not to underestimate you from now on."

Lilmit squared his bony shoulders. "Yes. You remember that, young lady. Someday we may even end up working on the same team."

Anja did not try to hide the genuine smile that sprang to her face. Things were working out even better than she had hoped. She had gotten her needed dose of spice, had discovered Czethros's true colors, and had already hatched a plan to make her former employer pay for at least some of his misdeeds.

With any luck she would also be able to keep the poor bumbling Lilmit out of harm's way while she carried out her plan. Perhaps Kessel would be the safest place for him. For now. She gave him a brisk nod. "No time to lose." She started to go, then turned back. "And Lilmit, whatever happens, don't let yourself be caught or hurt."

Lilmit nodded, misunderstanding her words. "Yes, I know how important the mission is. I won't let Czethros down. Just let me pack up and go now."

"Of course," Anja said. "I've got what I need. Thank you."

The man scuttled back into his craft and closed the door, sealing the hatch as if afraid she might follow him inside.

Anja looked around to make certain she wasn't being observed, and quickly took a dose of the precious spice.

More andris awaited her. She would go to Mon

Calamari and find the stash. But now that she realized she'd been betrayed and duped, it had become vital for her to foil Czethros's plans. She would keep only a small amount and destroy the rest, denying him that profit. She would ruin this scheme, just as she had helped destroy Lilmit's Anobis-bound weapons.

"You called me your little velker, Czethros," Anja purred in a low voice. "Now I'll show you just how unwise it is to get a velker angry!"

She clicked on her antique lightsaber, and the acid-yellow energy blade throbbed and sizzled. She ducked low, narrowing her huge eyes to see the workings of Lilmit's engines. She slashed quickly, severing two of the coolant lines in a sizzle of flashing sparks and smoking lubricants.

Lilmit might not notice immediately, but as he warmed up his engines in preparation for takeoff from Kessel, the engines would overheat and burn out. His craft would be stranded here, out of her way—and out of harm's way—for the duration of whatever was about to happen.

Before Czethros could set his plans in motion, Anja would be far away, putting *her* sabotage plans into effect on Mon Calamari.

At first, Czethros probably wouldn't even suspect who was doing this to him. But eventually he would learn.

Yes, eventually he would learn.

6

JAINA WAS SURPRISED at how good it felt to be in the pilot's seat of the *Rock Dragon* once again, even if they weren't exactly going on a fun trip. The pleasure of being surrounded by her best friends added fuel to the fire of her excitement as they set out on this new adventure.

"How's our navigator doing?" she asked, settling herself more comfortably in her seat, anxious to be off.

"Perfect," Zekk assured her. "Em Teedee's got the route and the timing to our first stop calculated down to the second."

"And naturally, I have been very thorough, as I always am when safety is concerned," Em Teedee preened. "You've come to expect only the best of me, and I should hate for your trust to be misplaced."

Jaina chuckled.

"Just give us the count, Em Teedee," Jacen urged. "We've got to go find Anja."

The little droid made a sound as if clearing its throat. "Prepare for transition to hyperspace in five, four, three, two . . ."

"Punch it, Lowie," Jaina said. Her ginger-furred copilot grumbled with satisfaction as he switched on the hyperdrive engines. Glittering stellar pinpricks exploded into brilliant starlines around them.

Jaina couldn't keep the smile of exhilaration off her face. "Isn't this exciting?"

"I'd be a lot more excited if I didn't feel responsible for the situation Anja's in," said Jacen.

Jaina swiveled in the pilot's seat to give her twin brother a strange look. "Responsible? How? We didn't have anything to do with Anja getting addicted to spice."

"Well, if Dad hadn't killed her father, maybe she'd've had parents to teach her right from wrong. She might never have gotten hooked on andris in the first place."

Jaina bristled. "I don't believe Dad shot Gallandro in the back, no matter what Anja says. *She* can't even be sure what happened. It's not as if she was there."

"Neither were we," Jacen pointed out. He sighed and rubbed the back of his neck. "Anyhow, it's not just Anja I'm worried about. I mean, we're heading for Kessel. I've got kind of a bad feeling about this."

Lowie smoothed the fur at the back of his neck and gave a thoughtful rumble.

"Have you sensed something through the Force?" Tenel Ka asked.

Jaina glanced back at her brother. He shrugged. "Not exactly, but Dad and Chewie sure had a hard time of it when they crashed on Kessel years ago."

Jaina turned and looked back out the front viewport. "It was hard for them to get away, but that was back when the spice mines were a slave pit. Dad reminds us whenever he gets a chance that Lando and Uncle Luke had to disguise themselves in order to sneak in and help him and Chewie escape." She bit her lower lip. "Now that Lando owns the mines, though, we shouldn't need to worry about anything."

"It's still not a place I'd like to go for a vacation," Zekk muttered.

"Hey, don't worry about it too much," Jacen said. "I told you, I didn't really sense anything through the Force. I'd just be extra careful when we land there."

Jaina nodded, but a frown of concern still wrinkled her brow.

"Such caution would be sensible," Tenel Ka agreed.

Once the *Rock Dragon* had landed near the spice mine's administrative offices on Kessel, a thin and dour-looking administrator arrived to greet them, introducing himself as Second Administrator Kymn.

"Your clearances are all in order," he said. "In fact, Master Skywalker himself sent a message asking for our cooperation in your mission— whatever it is. I'm to conduct you directly to the Chief Administrator's office. Nien Nunb is a very busy man."

The young Jedi Knights followed the sour-faced man. Jacen looked around at the bleak landscape and felt the barest hint of a tingle along the back of his neck, so faint he didn't think it could possibly be a warning through the Force. He scratched the back of his neck and tried to divert his thoughts.

"Well, I wouldn't exactly say we're on a mission," Jacen told the man. "We're just looking for someone. We won't take up much of his time."

The dour administrator looked suspiciously at him but said nothing as they entered the main administrative buildings. When they were finally led into the Chief Administrator's underground office, mousy little Nien Nunb got up, came around his low desk, and greeted each of them effusively, although they did not actually know one another. Em Teedee promptly provided translation services, since Nien Nunb's Basic was difficult to understand.

"Master Nien Nunb would like to thank you all for taking the time for this visit. He deems it a great honor that the relatives of his old friends Han Solo and Chewbacca of Kashyyyk have come to visit, and extends you any help he can offer."

"Thanks," Jacen said. "Maybe if we could look at—"

Nien Nunb held up a hand for Jacen to pause, then turned to the sour-faced administrator and said a few short words in his own language. Em Teedee continued translating. "Master Nien Nunb says thank you, Second Administrator Kymn. He will not require your services any further."

Kymn's lips pressed into a thin, tight line, but he made no argument as he withdrew. Nien Nunb strode to the doorway, shut the heavy door, and pressed his ear against it for a moment. Then, to all of their surprise, he locked the door.

The Sullustan Chief Administrator spoke rapidly and spread his hands to indicate a cluster of cushioned repulsor benches in a group on one side of his rock-walled office. "Master Nien Nunb urges you to be seated, and he is now anxious to learn the nature of the business that has brought you all here."

The five young Jedi explained about their search for their friend Anja and how they had hoped to find her here on Kessel. Nien Nunb put a hand to his chin and shook his broad head while he replied. In translation, Em Teedee explained that the Chief Administrator had not seen the *Lightning Rod* and, since he had known old Peckhum a good many years, he believed he would have recognized the ship had it landed anywhere in the main docking domes. He had been very busy and very concerned, however, so he couldn't be sure.

"Is it possible that she might have managed to sneak past your security screens?" Jaina asked.

Jacen frowned at his sister for implying that Anja was trying to do something illegal on Kessel, but Nien Nunb was already answering.

"In the past, Master Nien Nunb would have assured you that very little could get past his security screens here on Kessel, and that he knew of all comings and goings on this planet," Em Teedee said. "But in recent months there have been some small . . . occurrences that have led him to believe that perhaps all is not as it seems here. Therefore, he has offered to put the full resources of Kessel's computer records at your disposal. You may also physically search for Mistress Anja if you believe that will be of any use. He only urges you to be extremely cautious."

Tenel Ka, always slightly suspicious, sat up straighter. "May I inquire what the source of your concern is?"

The Chief Administrator opened his small mouth under drooping folds of skin, closed it, opened it, and closed it again, as if he could not decide exactly what to say. Finally the story spilled out, and he described the "accident" from which he had barely escaped with his life, the blasts of carbonite and the suspected sabotage that had cost the life of Torvon, the predecessor to Second Administrator Kymn.

"Master Nien Nunb has ordered immediate

inspections and has implemented new safety systems in order to foster the appearance that he has no suspicions of anything at all sinister." The young Jedi Knights looked at each other, trying to decide how dangerous the spice mines might really be.

Em Teedee went on. "He does not wish anyone to know that he now suspects treachery, and is no longer certain which of his employees he can trust. As of yet, however, he has no solid proof. Therefore, in return for his assistance in helping you with your search for Anja, he requests that you remain alert to any signs of illegal activity, danger, or deceit."

Tenel Ka gave a curt nod, and her warrior braids swayed around her shoulders. From the corner of his eye, Jacen saw Zekk's hand go to the hilt of his newly constructed lightsaber.

Jacen nodded, acknowledging the gravity of the situation. "Sure, we can do that."

7

THEIR SEARCH FOR any sign of the *Lightning Rod* in Kessel's haphazard docking records was apparently fruitless. Lowie, Em Teedee, and Jaina had chased through even the most elusive of electronic notations, looking for aliases, last-minute substitutions on standard cargo runs, even any vessel that might have requested sight-seeing privileges. Anja and the *Lightning Rod* were nowhere to be found. Either she had failed to identify her ship, or she had never come there at all.

Meanwhile, Zekk pored over a hard-copy diagram of all usable docking facilities on the planet, both authorized and unauthorized. Tenel Ka, with Jacen beside her, studied a listing of docking authorizations in the past week. Many of the ships were unnamed or only partially listed.

Jacen was about to ask just what kind of clue she expected to find when the warrior girl nodded with satisfaction. "Ah."

"Aha?" Jacen asked, not knowing exactly what she had found.

Zekk hurried over from the computer console. "The *Lightning Rod*? Or at least a lead we can follow?"

"No, but something unusual, nonetheless. A ship we have encountered before, on our way to Anja's world of Anobis."

Zekk squinted down at the shimmering electronic page. "The *Rude Awakening*?"

Jaina looked up from her computer console and scratched her head. "Sounds familiar but I can't place it."

"Hey, wasn't that the name of the ship we bumped into not far from Ord Mantell, that gunrunner?" Jacen said.

Jaina frowned. "You mean Lilmit? But what would a gunrunner—or even an ex-gunrunner—be doing here on Kessel?"

With a thoughtful growl, Lowie began punching commands into the computer console. A moment later he gave a suspicious woof.

"Yes, indeed, Master Lowbacca. Very odd!" Em Teedee agreed. "It seems that our smuggling friend has a valid authorization to pick up a shipment here on Kessel." Lowie added something with a sharp bark. "Why, yes. Given the circumstances, I daresay he should have docked in one of the standard commercial loading bays."

"But he's not," Jaina observed. "According to

this code list, Lilmit's authorization came directly through Nien Nunb's late Second Administrator."

"So where is he docked then?" Zekk asked impatiently.

Jaina stood, leaned over Zekk's sheet of docking diagrams, and pointed. "A cargo bay way over here, near all the new andris-mining and processing operations. Perfectly legal, of course. Just . . . really out of the way."

"Sounds suspicious to me," Jacen admitted. "I don't think Anja actually knows this guy, but it seems like an awfully big coincidence that he *just happened* to be in the Anobis system when we were there, and now he *just happens* to be on Kessel."

Tenel Ka nodded. "Perhaps Nien Nunb's conspiracy theory has a more solid foundation than we realized."

"Hey, either way," Jacen said, "I'd say it's about time we paid our old smuggler friend Lilmit a visit."

Without saying a word as he came up from behind, Jacen put a hand on Lilmit's slumped shoulder. The onetime weapons smuggler, his head and neck buried in the engine compartment of the *Rude Awakening*, gave a start and banged his head.

"Anything we can help you with, Lilmit?" Jaina asked sweetly.

"What do you mean, sneaking up on a guy like that?" Lilmit muttered, backing up to extricate himself from the opening in the access panel.

Lowie gave a warning rumble. Lilmit whirled at

the sound, stumbled backward a step, and hit his head again, this time on the outside of the engine compartment.

"No, no, it can't be!" the hapless man said, staring around at the semicircle of faces he had not seen since his disastrous weapons smuggling assignment to Anobis. "Not you, too! I'm ruined. Why can't everyone just leave me alone?" Lilmit squeezed his eyes shut. "Please let me go. I was just about to leave."

Exchanging amused glances, Jaina and Lowie popped their heads inside the engine compartment to take a look. Jaina withdrew again and gave Lilmit a skeptical look. "From the looks of your engines, I don't think you're going anywhere soon."

Lowie's roar echoed inside the engine compartment. "Master Lowbacca confirms this diagnosis," Em Teedee translated.

Jaina placed her hands on her hips. "Even if Kessel does have all the replacement parts you need, it'll take a pair of skilled mechanics *two days* to get this mess fixed."

Lilmit blanched. "Days? I don't have days. I don't even have any credits. I need to leave before Kessel is—" He clamped his mouth shut. His eyes darted from side to side as he fluttered his hands, spreading his webbed fingers. "I, uh, have to leave today. Is there any way I might persuade you to help me?"

"Why?" Jacen asked sourly. "So you can deliver

some more weapons to desperate people in war zones?"

The former arms smuggler drew himself up haughtily. "I'm not *in* that line of business anymore." He blinked rapidly. "I—I'm completely legitimate now."

Tenel Ka raised an eyebrow. "Transporting spice, perhaps?"

Lilmit looked defensive. His nostrils flared. "Yes, a small, *authorized* shipment. And it's . . . urgently needed."

"Ah," Jacen said.

"Aha," Tenel Ka finished, nodding gravely.

"So you see," Lilmit said defensively, "you mustn't interfere with my business anymore. I'm on an errand of . . . mercy."

"Actually, we're not here to interfere with you at all," Zekk said, stepping forward a bit. "We're looking for some information about a friend of ours. You see, our friend . . . borrowed my ship, the *Lightning Rod*."

Jacen could sense Zekk's struggle to come up with an explanation that would not involve lying. His emerald-green eyes clouded for a moment, then cleared. "We had planned to rendezvous at the first stop, but our friend obviously got here first and didn't wait."

The story was true, Jacen thought admiringly. The young Jedi had hoped to meet Anja here. Anja herself had not known this, though, and so of course had not waited for them.

"I don't know. I haven't seen her," Lilmit protested. "Or that hunk of junk she was flying."

Her, Jacen thought, and *that hunk of junk*. So Anja and the *Lightning Rod* had been here. It was fortunate for the young Jedi Knights that Lilmit was such a poor liar. The fellow was obviously desperate to get away. There was no doubt left in Jacen's mind now that the former gunrunner had not only seen Anja, but had spoken to her as well. He could sense it strongly through the Force.

Jacen moved closer to Lilmit and spoke in a confidential tone. "Look, we already know Anja was here in the *Lightning Rod*." He had only known this for a few seconds, but Lilmit didn't need to be told that. "She desperately needs our help with something she's trying to do," he continued in a low voice. At least, Jacen *thought* Anja was trying to give up using spice. From everything Lando had told them and from what Jacen had seen so far, Anja would need her friends' help to get through this.

"We were sent here to help her," Jaina added in a persuasive tone. She sighed with feigned resignation. "But if you don't know anything, you don't. It's a shame, too. The Chief Administrator of this facility owes us a favor and probably would have been more than happy to give us a few rather hard-to-find engine parts that you could have used to fix your ship."

Jacen shrugged, turning to go. "Well, good luck anyway, Lilmit. I'm sure you'll understand we're in kind of a hurry." He took a stab in the dark. "We'll just have to hope we link up with her at the next rendezvous before it's too late."

Lilmit swallowed convulsively but did not speak.

"You do understand, do you not, that we were sent to assist Anja Gallandro *with the spice*?" Tenel Ka said, leaning close to Lilmit, a meaningful look in her cool gray eyes.

Lilmit's eyes went wide as comprehension dawned. Jacen was pretty sure Lilmit didn't know they'd been sent by Master Skywalker, and therefore he had no idea what sense Lilmit might have made out of Tenel Ka's cryptic comment, but he was aware that the warrior girl had an intricate understanding of deceptions, plots, and conspiracies. Somehow, Jacen thought in admiration, she had known just what to say.

Jaina added a last little push. "Well, there's no time to lose. We may as well get going and just hope we can rendezvous with her at Ord Mantell. . . ."

Jacen saw no answering flicker of confirmation in Lilmit's eyes.

"Or," Jaina went on, "Coruscant . . . ?"

"No!" Lilmit practically yelped. "Calamari! She's gone to Mon Calamari." He lowered his voice to a whisper. "The Coruscant assignment is *mine*."

Jacen tried to clear his mind. They were getting answers, but he had no idea what they were talking about! He hoped someone knew.

Lilmit seemed to warm up to them now. "I was testing you, of course. For Anja. You can never be too sure about these things," he said, nodding several times. "Especially since you interfered with my shipment to Anobis. I got into a lot of trouble for that."

"We had our reasons," Zekk broke in, "but we'd like to make it up to you now."

Lilmit smiled. "You're sure you can get me the engine parts I need?"

"Of course—nothing simpler," Jaina assured him smoothly.

Lowie rumbled a curt suggestion. "Master Lowbacca advises you to talk first," Em Teedee translated. "Then we will see to getting your parts."

"But you'll have to do the engine work yourself," Jaina warned. "We've got our own mission."

Lilmit nodded. "Fair enough. Just as long as I get off of this rock . . . in time."

8

AS A JEDI, Jaina felt bound by her promises, no matter whom she made them to, and so once they got back to Chief Administrator's cozy underground office, the first order of business was to make sure Lilmit got the promised engine parts. Once that was taken care of, Nien Nunb listened carefully to their description of the encounter with the former gunrunner.

The Sullustan touched a finger to his layered lips and murmured thoughtfully. Em Teedee was proud to offer an immediate translation. "Master Nien Nunb believes that Lilmit's urgent desire to leave Kessel before some mysterious deadline indicates that some conspiracy is indeed afoot."

"Does seem to kind of support your theory that something's going on, Nien Nunb," Jaina agreed. "But we have no idea *what*. Lilmit's anxiety could be something perfectly simple."

"Or perhaps not," Tenel Ka said ominously. "We must be prepared."

Lowie roared, and the little droid responded rather than translating. "Oh, indeed, Master Lowbacca, we mustn't leave Master Nien Nunb unprotected here in the spice mines. He can trust *us*, of course, but otherwise he has no idea who his friends or his enemies might be."

"All right. So we'll have to leave someone here while the rest of us go look for our friend," Jaina said. "Zekk?"

He gave a vigorous shake of his head. "Anja has the *Lightning Rod*. I'm not going to stay here while the rest of you go after her."

Jaina frowned but had to admit the logic of this. She knew better than to get between a being and his ship. "Jacen, how about you?"

Her brother gave her an "Oh, come on!" type of look. "Jaina, if Anja trusts anybody, it's me. I can't leave her out there to face her problems all alone."

Jaina's heart sank. She couldn't really ask Tenel Ka to stay here and let Zekk and Jacen go flying off in her ship, the *Rock Dragon*. She turned toward her last hope. "Lowie?" she said in a weak voice.

Lowie slapped a ginger-furred hand on her back and rumbled something consoling.

"An excellent idea, Mistress Jaina," Em Teedee said. "Master Lowbacca and I should be delighted to stay here with you and er, um . . . protect the interests of Master Nien Nunb."

Jaina gave an unconvincing smile. "Right." She

hadn't really wanted to stay here herself, but she couldn't argue the matter now.

Zekk put an arm around her shoulder, leaned close, and whispered, "Thanks for understanding."

Jaina snorted. Zekk kissed her playfully on the cheek and said, "By the way, is it my turn to rescue you this time, or the other way around?"

Jaina pretended to glare at him until he kissed her on the other cheek. He grinned. "Don't worry. If you need me, I'll be back."

Jaina slid both arms around his waist to hug him tightly. She pressed her cheek against Zekk's, whispered, "May the Force be with you," and then let go.

With Zekk as pilot, Jacen as copilot, and Tenel Ka as navigator, the trio set off for Mon Calamari in the *Rock Dragon*. Jacen was interested to see that Zekk looked much more relaxed when he was piloting a starship. He could sense that his dark-haired friend used the Force unconsciously to help him maneuver, judge distances, and react to small emergencies.

Jacen's spirits were rising too, not only because he enjoyed doing something useful during a flight, but also because Tenel Ka was there working beside him. And because they had found a solid lead as to Anja's whereabouts.

"Jacen, my friend, did you not say you knew someone who could assist us on Mon Calamari?" Tenel Ka said once they were well under way.

"Right. Her name is Ambassador Cilghal. Guess

I ought to send her a message to see if she's there right now and if she has time to work with us."

"Cilghal?" Zekk said. "Didn't she used to be a student of Master Skywalker's, back in the early days of the academy?"

Tenel Ka looked interested. "She is a Jedi *and* an Ambassador?"

"Yeah. A Jedi healer and an Ambassador. The only one that I've heard of, so far," Jacen said. "But Cilghal is so quiet and gentle, you'd never know she has all that power."

For the next few minutes he busied himself sending a communiqué that explained their current mission and requested Cilghal's help. Moments after the *Rock Dragon* dropped out of hyperspace into the Calamari system, they received the Ambassador's answer.

According to the message, it would be Ambassador Cilghal's greatest pleasure to assist them, and she had already begun making inquiries about recent arrivals on the planet to track down the *Lightning Rod*. She had also set up the appropriate clearances and approvals for the *Rock Dragon* to have a berth in the VIP docking section near her offices on Foamwander City for as many days as the young Jedi Knights might need it.

Tenel Ka looked impressed. "It would seem that Ambassador Cilghal is most efficient."

A lopsided grin brightened Jacen's face. "Yeah, she thinks of everything."

"Good," Zekk said. "You think there's any chance

she'll have the *Lighting Rod* waiting for us by the time we land?"

Jacen rolled his eyes. "Even *I'm* not that optimistic."

Tenel Ka reached over to pat Zekk on the shoulder with her single hand. "It is important to keep one's hopes up."

In less than an hour, the *Rock Dragon* was docked in the VIP area of Cilghal's beautiful floating metropolis of Foamwander City. The Ambassador herself met them as they disembarked from the small Hapan passenger cruiser on one of the mist-dampened upper decks. Jacen made the introductions, and the female Calamarian greeted him and his friends with all the warmth of a proud aunt.

Cilghal was a gentle-voiced member of the fish-like race that also included the famous Admiral Ackbar. She wore watery blue robes that seemed to ripple and change color like the tides of the sea. Her blunt, salmon-colored head was streaked with a flush of pale green. She raised a massive flipperlike hand in greeting.

With the formalities over, Cilghal led them to a beautiful private dining area. Handing each of them a datapad into which the week's arrivals from off-planet had been downloaded, she excused herself and ordered them all some food: salted fish, seaweed rolls, and something moist and delicious that they plucked out of scrolled shells.

Before they had finished their midday meal, the young Jedi Knights had tracked down not only the point and time of Anja's arrival, but also the city to which she had moved herself and the *Lightning Rod* the evening before. The location was far to the north, in the ice-choked waters of the arctic circle.

"Crystal Reef!" Cilghal said with surprise when they showed her their findings. "A vacation resort reserved only for the wealthy and elite. If you wish to go there, I had better get to work immediately. *Everybody* wants to go to Crystal Reef, and even the planet's Ambassador to the New Republic doesn't necessarily get preferential treatment."

Three hours later, they found themselves at Foamwander City's water docks with all arrangements made for their trip north to Crystal Reef. The three young Jedi walked behind Cilghal as she led them to her waveskimmer.

"Most efficient," Tenel Ka stated again with obvious approval, looking at the Ambassador and her sleek watercraft.

Cilghal crossed the gangplank, boarded the skimmer, and began a safety check. "How does she do it?" Jacen wondered aloud.

"Cilghal is amazing, all right," Zekk agreed, walking across the narrow plank and stepping down into the skimmer. Jacen went next. The seas were choppy and the little boat dipped and swayed beneath him. Far below, he could discern shadowy forms swimming just barely out of sight. He turned to offer a hand to help Tenel Ka across. But with a mischievous glint in her eye, Tenel Ka ignored his hand, ignored the plank and the railing. In a single bound, she jumped aboard.

9

JUST ANOTHER DAY at the spice mines of Kessel.

The routine went as usual: transports came in, packages were marked, cargo was unloaded and shipped off under carefully observed transport restrictions. Nien Nunb had established rigid protocols and accounting methods to be sure that all spice orders were watched and sold to the properly authorized customers. Nothing could ever be perfect, but he knew the setup was as efficient as that of any other business in the sector.

The small Sullustan sat in his deep control chamber, overseeing the daily business of his spice mines. He was surrounded by several important business associates and administrators, as well as his hired mercenary guards. So far he had managed to keep from panicking about the attempt on his life, and it made him confident to know that Han Solo's children and their Jedi friends were investigating the "accident." But how many henchmen did Torvon have hidden here in the mines? And who did they really work for?

In fact, Jaina, Lowbacca, and their translating droid were even now out scouting for evidence of untoward activities and trying to find clues as to what was really going on. Nien Nunb had had to trade a few engine parts for the news that something was going to happen here on Kessel, but it was a small price to pay for the knowledge that he did, indeed, need to stay alert.

His new right-hand man, Second Administrator Kymn, moved toward the transport control deck. The screen showed a string of lights that indicated all approaching craft, all scheduled arrivals, and all major navigational hazards from the debris of Kessel's exploded garrison moon.

"Administrator Nunb, we have a large cargo transport arriving from Ord Mantell. Exactly on schedule, sir," Kymn said.

The mousy Chief Administrator blinked his huge watery eyes and leaned closer to the display. Nien Nunb could not recall any expected arrival of such an enormous cargo ship. He jabbered quickly, since Second Administrator Kymn understood the Sullustan's language.

"Oh, yes, Administrator Nunb. This was set up weeks ago," Kymn answered. "That transport is carrying the new office furniture, as well as food supplies, life-support recharge packs, and atmosphere enrichment generators. Don't you remember signing the requisitions?"

Nien Nunb still had no recollection of the ship's impending arrival, but he squinted at the screen again and saw that everything seemed to be in order. In fact, the craft had already descended through Kessel's wispy atmosphere and was even now approaching the opening doors of the central cargo bay.

Nien Nunb blinked in surprise. Normally, such a transport would be routed to the supply annex.

Second Administrator Kymn pointed to a list of heavy items on the cargo manifest. "I felt it would be more efficient to bring him into the main loading bay where we have our best equipment to handle large cargo."

The Sullustan mumbled his agreement, though a quiet uneasiness had begun to work in his abdomen. His instincts urged him to crawl into a dark tunnel and hide where he knew he would be safe.

Kymn touched a communicator stud in his ear, listened for a moment, and then said, "Acknowledged." He turned to Nien Nunb with a smile. "The captain requests that you come to greet him personally. He's something of an amateur historian of the Rebellion against the Empire, and he would be honored to meet you and get your autograph."

The Sullustan beamed and stood up, chattering with surprise.

"Yes, I'm certain of it. He wants to shake the hand of the man who flew copilot with Lando

Calrissian at the destruction of the second Death Star."

The Chief Administrator burbled with pleasure, but insisted that they bring guards along, just in case. Kymn agreed and pointed to three of the guards in the control room, naming them specifically. "Come with us."

Together, they all marched down to the main cargo bay. They put on breathing masks before going into the docking area, which was now open to the thin, cold air of Kessel so that the cargo ship could enter. Nien Nunb stood beside his secondary administrator. The guards flanked him on either side, while another hovered close in the rear.

The cargo ship landed. Its markings were from a private Ord Mantell trading company. Nien Nunb thought the spice mines had dealt with that trading firm before, but couldn't be sure. This bothered him, because normally his memory for that sort of detail was quite reliable. Perhaps his anxiety from the assassination attempt had disturbed him more than he'd suspected.

The exit hatch on the cargo ship hissed open, and the captain swung out. He had tousled blond hair, a freckled face, and bright blue eyes that fixed instantly on the Sullustan manager. When the captain smiled, his teeth flashed so white it looked like starfire. "Nien Nunb! Boy, am I glad to meet you!"

The Sullustan stepped forward on his small feet, pleased at such recognition. The grinning blond captain pumped his small, rodentlike hand and then turned back to his cargo ship. "I knew I was coming to your place, Chief Administrator Nunb, sir, so I wanted to bring a special surprise. I hope you don't mind. Here, follow me so you can watch me open up my cargo doors. You're not going to believe this."

The captain worked the controls to release the large doors covering the craft's cargo bay. Second Administrator Kymn stepped close to Nien Nunb, as if eager to observe his surprise. The three hand-picked guards they had brought along stationed themselves at strategic points in the bay.

When the cargo ship's doors cracked open, Nien Nunb saw movement. Startled, he took half a step back. A split second later, armed mercenary fighters boiled out of the cargo ship, shouting, weapons drawn.

A nearby guard planted his blaster rifle against the Chief Administrator's back.

Feeling the cold muzzle pressing between his shoulder blades, the Sullustan squawked and raised his hands. More mercenaries charged down the ship's ramp, leaping into the cargo chamber and firing their weapons into the air. Within an instant they had created massive confusion and havoc.

Second Administrator Kymn drew his own weapon, a holdout blaster, and turned to fire a shot at one of the other guards who stood over by the communications array. The surprised man flew backward into the wall.

The remaining two guards who had come from

the comm and control center also opened fire. Nien Nunb thought for a moment they might defend him and repel the attackers. But instead the guards—his own guards!—joined the newcomers, adding their strength to this surprising coup in the spice mines of Kessel.

Gunfire ricocheted off the walls, rattling the insulation plates. The mousy Sullustan tried to duck out of the way. He wondered how long this turmoil would go on. As he blinked and looked around, he saw that the brilliant smile on the blond pilot's face now held a wicked edge. Nien Nunb had been deceived—completely deceived.

He had no choice but to surrender.

Continuing their investigation through the winding tunnels, Jaina and Lowie trudged after the miniaturized translating droid as he floated along following a map of the mine catacombs he had downloaded earlier.

"I've got a strong feeling that something's gone wrong," Jaina said. "But we haven't found a thing yet."

Lowie growled his agreement, and they used their Jedi senses in an attempt to pinpoint where the crisis would occur. They emerged at the edge of a shaft that opened on the upper wall of the central control and cargo bay—just as blaster fire erupted ahead of them.

"Oh, my!" Em Teedee said. "Take cover quickly!

What if a blaster bolt ricochets up here? We're doomed!"

"Jedi Knights don't hide in a crisis," Jaina said. Lowie growled and reached for his lightsaber, ready to push forward, but Jaina held him back. "On the other hand, looks like an entire military force down there. We're heavily outgunned. Wouldn't do any good to jump into that mess without a plan. We'd be captured or killed in seconds."

Lowie groaned his acquiescence.

"You show admirable restraint, Mistress Jaina," Em Teedee said.

They looked down and watched helplessly. Within minutes, the mercenary soldiers had subdued all resistance with as little bloodshed as possible.

"Put the element of surprise to good use, didn't they? A complete takeover." Jaina narrowed her eyes and glared down at the turncoat guards and Second Administrator Kymn, knowing that this treachery must have been planned for some time. She also recalled the members of the Wing Guard on Cloud City, who had turned traitor and sold out to Black Sun. Something was definitely going on at the fringes of the New Republic—something big.

Kymn ran to the intercom on the wall, pressed the transmit button, and shouted, "Signal Alpha! Signal Alpha!" Then he went back to take his position, proudly holding his blaster pistol.

"I do believe that must be some sort of code," Em Teedee said. Lowie grumbled for the little droid to be quiet so as not to give away their position.

Second Administrator Kymn, wearing a superior smile now, spoke quickly to the Chief Administrator. "Our allies are in place at every important station on Kessel. We have just finished taking over all the control points. I hope our people were able to assert themselves without too many deaths. The important thing is that they're well armed and prepared to do what's necessary. Don't doubt it."

Fresh soldiers continued to file out of the large cargo ship.

"It's an entire occupation force," Jaina whispered.

The invaders brought out heavy equipment, weapons, and supplies. Forming rows, the mercenary troops looked on attentively as a tall shadow moved inside the cargo hold. Jaina gasped with recognition as the towering man stepped into the light. Sickly pale skin contrasted with close-cropped moss-green hair. A thin metallic visor sported a dark red cyber-eye that glinted, shifting constantly from one side to the other.

"Lord Czethros!" Administrator Kymn said. "Welcome to the spice mines of Kessel. Our takeover is complete. This facility is now yours."

Czethros strode down, square-shouldered and proud, as if there had never been any question of ownership in his mind. "Excellent job," he said. "Kessel will become my new base of operations. From here we will coordinate our lightning strikes— multiple covert attacks just like this one, only on a much larger scale. I'm glad our plan here operated so efficiently. A good sign."

He smiled, and his mercenaries beamed at the praise. Jaina knew that Czethros was not a man to give compliments easily.

"In a similar manner, all of our infiltrators in key positions in important systems will be able to strike as soon as we transmit the signal for our coordinated takeovers. The attacks will be simultaneous. Within days we will bring the New Republic to its knees. Black Sun will prevail!"

He raised a fist in the air, and the other mercenaries shouted in unison, "Black Sun!"

"Dear me! Whatever are we going to do?" Em Teedee said as Jaina and Lowie backed deeper into the shadows of the tunnel.

"Well, there's one good thing about all of this so far," Jaina said, her face grim and determined. "We're Jedi Knights—and Czethros doesn't know that we're here."

10

PILOTED BY CILGHAL, the waveskimmer roared across the choppy seas toward the polar oceans of Mon Calamari. The sky was steely gray, the water cold. Mountainous icebergs floated in the distance like broken white teeth jutting up from the surface of the waves. The air felt so frigid that it seemed it might break if they tore through it too quickly.

"There, those sparkling colors," Jacen said, pointing. "Is that Crystal Reef?"

Cilghal nodded. "Crystal Reef is one of the most popular casino-resorts on all of Mon Calamari."

Protruding from the waves and surrounded by an archipelago of icebergs was an artificial island, a glittering mound of lights and metal that drifted about on the frigid currents. The Crystal Reef casino-resort was incredibly exclusive, isolated, a place for the wealthiest members of any species to go and have fun.

Zekk shivered, even wrapped in his warm cloak. "Why would anyone want to come up here? It's too cold to relax."

Tenel Ka, clad only in her lizard-hide armor, seemed unaffected by the drop in temperature or the brisk salty spray that feathered up from the racing waveskimmer.

"Wait until you see Crystal Reef from the inside," Cilghal said, her voice soft, the words rich. "If I weren't an ambassador to my people, we would have had to wait a month simply to get docking privileges. I . . . pulled a great many strings."

"Then how did Anja Gallandro manage to get here?" Tenel Ka said.

Jacen raised his eyebrows and looked over at her. "You should know by now not to underestimate Anja when she's determined to do something."

Cilghal brought the waveskimmer into a crowded VIP docking area that looked like a series of metal-ceilinged caverns at the floating island's water level. Expertly, she wove her way between other bobbing vessels—many of them jewel-spangled or gaudily painted—and nudged the skimmer into place. Jacen, Tenel Ka, and Zekk scrambled out onto the well-lighted dock, while the Calamarian ambassador filled out the proper forms and punched in her access codes.

Jacen gazed upward, lifting his chin so he could see the pearly metallic ceiling, the curved girders that supported the casino-resort's organic, flow-form architecture. The style reminded him of the

strange coral reef design he'd seen the Mon Calamarians use in the designs of their world's impres-
sive star cruisers.

A surprising variety of beings bustled about,
many of them obviously tourists, others uniformed
employees of the Crystal Reef resort. Jacen noticed
Mon Calamarians, tenacled Quarren, Bith musi-
cians, walrus-faced Aqualish, horned Devaronians,
and ten other races of sentient creatures he could
identify, as well as two dozen more he could not.

Layered musical tones filled the air like scents,
ranging from rumbling subsonic pulses, through
music discernible by human ears, up into high-
pitched frequencies that he could detect only as a
faint vibration in his teeth.

"Crystal Reef is a large place in which to find a
single person," Tenel Ka said.

Cilghal spoke in her soothing voice. "Fortunately, the resort has no choice but to allow me
access to its records."

"Then we should be able to track Anja through
the resort's own computer systems," Zekk said, in a
determined tone. "She doesn't seem to be trying as
hard to cover her tracks here. We'll find her—and
the *Lightning Rod*, I hope. I miss my ship."

Jacen continued to defend her. "I don't think
she's necessarily been hiding from us. Anja obviously needs to do something quickly, and is trying
to do it before anyone gets in the way."

"She still stole my ship . . . ," Zekk grumbled.
"And she might have guessed we'd come after her."

"We'll ask her when we find her," Cilghal said and led them up into the main levels of the resort. After consulting some maps on the walls, the Mon Calamarian ambassador asked for guidance from uniformed attendants. Even she had not been to this place before. The courteous and helpful attendants answered every question.

On different levels in the floating city, temperatures and atmospheric compositions varied from cold and clammy to hot and dry environments. In some, Jacen could smell acrid sulfurous gases; in others the air seemed so fresh and pristine he wanted to take huge gulps of it and wished he could save some for later.

The support columns in the vaulted rooms were hollow water-filled cylinders made of transparisteel. Seaweeds, water flowers, and brightly colored fishes drifted from level to level through the connecting tubes.

Finally, after ascending several ramps and sliding stairs, they reached the upper decks of Crystal Reef, high above the glittering, ice-choked water. Out in the frigid air, Jacen watched cold puffs of fog rise up in front of his face each time he exhaled. Chattering Bothans played a game by sliding colorful tiles across a frost-slick surface.

Steaming hot tubs bubbled at the center of the deck, their warm vapors rising a few meters before condensing into icicles on the deck railings and nearby furniture. Inside the tubs lizardlike aliens basked in the incredible liquid heat. Jacen could feel the increased temperature hovering over them like a steamy atmosphere dome.

Meanwhile, Dralls frolicked in the water of the polar ocean below, their dark, short fur protecting them from the freezing temperatures. He watched them splash and play, having the time of their lives in the icy waves.

"Do you think Anja would be on one of the casino decks?" Zekk asked.

Tenel Ka frowned. "We can rule out no possibility."

Jacen shook his head. He looked behind him at the tall white towers glistening like spikes above the floating city. All legal forms of gambling were practiced on Crystal Reef—from races to simple games to major sabacc tournaments. Jacen wanted none of that, and he had to believe that Anja Gallandro didn't either.

"I doubt gambling has anything to do with why Anja came here. If she wanted to gamble, she could have done plenty on Cloud City—but she didn't show any interest then. No, she came to Mon Calamari for some other reason after leaving Kessel. Maybe she was looking for someone she knows. In any case, we'll just have to find out what she really had in mind."

"You forget, Jacen, my friend," Tenel Ka said, "if she is connected with Black Sun, they would wish to control all the gambling here. Therefore, her contacts may be on the gambling levels. This is a fact."

Jacen had to concede the point, but it still didn't sound right to him.

Finally, Cilghal found an information kiosk studded with computers and keyboards fitted for various types of tentacles, claws, and manipulative digits. She spoke quickly but politely to the data-hunter at the kiosk, a small-boned creature with ten articulated arms. Cilghal gave her diplomatic credentials and described the person they were seeking.

The data-hunter's smooth, toothless mouth smiled politely. Its numerous arms and hands moved in a blur, typing in requests, searching records, hunting through databases. "Ah, what excellent luck, Ambassador. Anja Gallandro should be easy to locate in our beautiful city," the data-hunter said. "The young lady has not yet visited any of our casinos or gaming establishments, though with *your* good luck, Ambassador, maybe you should."

Jacen tried unsuccessfully to suppress a chuckle at this blatant sales pitch. When Cilghal did not answer, the data-hunter quickly continued. "In fact, your friend has run up only a minimal bill during her stay here. Perhaps she is on the budget plan?"

"That is a strong possibility," Tenel Ka confirmed.

"Wouldn't surprise me a bit," Zekk muttered.

Impatient to get going, Jacen leaned forward. "So where is she now?"

"Ah." The data-hunter looked down at the screen, though Jacen could see only a blur of symbols flashing by. "At this moment, Anja Gallandro is visiting in our popular vehicle-rental docks attempting to procure a highly enjoyable underwater mode of transportation. I see . . . she has been there for some time already. I believe she is engaged in an energetic discussion with our fine entertainment representative.

"Unfortunately, your friend has no reservation or established credit, and we have quite a long and enthusiastic waiting list. Our state-of-the-art mini-submersibles are one of the most sought-after forms of entertainment here on beautiful Crystal Reef. I could book one for you, if you are interested, Ambassador. We have a spectacular brochure. . . ." The data-hunter reached out an articulated hand to offer them a packet of colorful images.

But Cilghal turned away with a polite smile. "Thank you. You've been most helpful." Giving a friendly wave, she ushered her young Jedi friends toward a lift platform behind the information booth. The data-hunter raised all ten arms in a shrug of dismay and waited for another customer from whom it could earn a commission.

They descended again to water level, where durasteel arches opened out onto the cold oceans, letting some of the waves drift in, lapping against the supports. The structure of the Crystal Reef casino-resort muffled the water's extreme choppiness.

A slow moving, treelike Yarin stood at the water's edge with its root-feet dangling into the water. The Yarin blocked access to all the rows of parked watercraft and minisubs. Anja stood there arguing with him, looking frustrated and weary, as if she'd been through the same phrases time and again. Her body seemed to tremble, but whether it was from tension or fatigue or something else, Jacen couldn't tell. A line of customers waited behind her, glowering.

Jacen saw her and ran forward, accompanied by Zekk. "Anja! Hey, am I glad to see you!"

"You weren't too easy to find," Zekk added.

The young woman whirled and snatched the lightsaber handle from her waist. Her huge eyes opened wide at seeing the young Jedi Knights. Her face flushed, and her hand shook slightly as she released her grip on the lightsaber, but in a moment she recovered her arrogant demeanor. She tossed her head so that her long flowing hair drifted back behind her shoulders. "Good. I'm glad you're here. Will you tell this . . . this *tree stump* here, who seems to have wood for brains, that I need to get a submersible, and I need it *now*?"

"Perhaps I could be of assistance," Cilghal said, gliding forward in her rippling blue robes, "*if* you would explain to us why you need it. But not otherwise."

Anja crossed her arms over her chest, flashing her dark tattoo. "And who are you? Another one of these Mon Calamarian casino employees trying to push me around?"

"I am Cilghal," she said, nodding patiently and

rolling her round brown eyes. "I am a Jedi Knight, and the ambassador for this planet."

"Oh," Anja said, somewhat flustered. "I . . . I'm pleased to meet you."

"What purpose will a submersible craft serve?" Tenel Ka asked. "We have already found you here. Do you need to escape again?"

"And where's my ship?" Zekk asked pointedly. "You'd better have taken care of the *Lightning Rod*."

"Not a scratch," Anja said. "And I would have returned it, if you'd given me time. I just . . . needed to get some transportation in a hurry."

"I'm listening," Zekk said, still skeptical. "But you're not explaining very much."

"Why should I have to explain everything to you?" Anja said, her voice uncharacteristically shaky. "I've got my own problems."

"You stole my ship, for one thing," Zekk retorted. "I'd say that deserves some explanation."

"Hey, if you want our help," Jacen said, trying to calm them both down, "maybe a few answers would make things easier. Come on, give us a break, Anja. We're your friends."

The young woman sighed, then stalked away from the treelike Yarin, who seemed entirely unfazed by the confrontation. The other customers came forward, relieved to have their turn at last.

A frown wrinkling her brow, Anja sat down on a damp bench and put her chin in her hands. "This is humiliating." Tears formed in her enormous eyes, but she didn't let them fall. "I found out that I've been a fool." Jacen blinked in surprise to hear such an unexpected admission from the disturbed young woman. "Your friend Lando Calrissian was right: I . . . I'm addicted to spice.

"I told you I could quit whenever I chose to. I believed it myself. Then I tried to quit. That was when I learned I'd only been fooling myself. I went to Kessel to get another dose, and it was there that I discovered the extent of my foolishness. I've been betrayed."

"Not by us," Jacen assured her, an anxious expression on his face.

"No," Anja said in a heavy voice.

"Who do you know on Kessel?" Zekk asked. "And why did you go there in the first place?"

"Black Sun has been controlling me," she said with a bitter laugh. "And I didn't even know it. Czethros acted as if he was my friend. He helped me when I needed it. He gave me food and supplies and training when I was just a desperate street kid. He gave me all the andris spice I wanted. I wouldn't have had a career piloting small ships without him."

"But . . . Czethros?" Jacen said, aghast. "He's a criminal, a murderer—"

"Czethros is an evil man," Tenel Ka said. "He is in hiding and the entire New Republic is searching for him."

"I'm out to get even with him, too," Anja said. "He lied to me. He said he had my best interests at heart. I trusted him, but now I know that behind my back *he* was selling those terrible weapons to perpetuate the civil war on Anobis. *He's* the one responsible for so many years of hopelessness, so much suffering, so much death. He used me. And I *allowed* it to happen. . . ."

She shuddered, then looked up at Jacen, Zekk, and Tenel Ka. Her face grew ruddy with anger and embarrassment. "But not anymore. Czethros is involved in spice smuggling, you know. He also controls the gambling in hot spots throughout the galaxy, and he's engineering a major takeover. He's got operatives—traitors—in positions of importance everywhere. There's no way the New Republic can stop him."

She flashed a humorless smile. "But I know a way to hurt him." She looked back toward the submersibles. "He has a large stash of andris spice here, under the Calamarian ice caps."

"Makes sense," Zekk said. "That would keep the andris cold, and intensify its effects."

"It's been delivered from Kessel in small shipments and stored there. Black Sun dealers will start distributing it to some of the high-rolling gambler clientele here soon . . . unless I can destroy it first."

Tenel Ka frowned skeptically. "If you are addicted to spice, why should you be eager to destroy it?"

"Because it'll hurt Czethros."

"And you're sure you won't just save a little for yourself?" Zekk challenged.

"You can come with me if you want," Anja said defiantly. "In fact, I could use your help to get past that stupid tree-man. I've got to rent a minisub. We can go together, find the stash, and destroy it. I guarantee that'll deflate some of Czethros's plans."

"But why do we not take the spice back to doctors and patients who need it?" Tenel Ka asked.

"Because some of Czethros's men may already be on their way to stop me. If we don't destroy that spice, I have no doubt Czethros will manage to put his hands on it again before we ever have a chance to get it safely away from Mon Calamari."

Jacen looked at Zekk and Tenel Ka. "It would be a pretty safe way to strike a blow against him—and with all those credits lost, it would really hurt." He glanced back at Anja. "Was Czethros behind the troubles we had on Cloud City?"

She hung her head. "Yes . . . and I didn't do a thing to stop him. At the time, I still wouldn't let myself trust you. Even so, I had no idea he would try to have you murdered. Please believe me."

"Sure, but why *didn't* you trust us? We've tried to be friends to you in every way," Jacen said, still surprised.

"Yes, but you're also the son of Han Solo. I was hoping that you might still prove yourself to be as cowardly and untrustworthy as your father." Anja's eyes did not meet his. Despite the cold, perspiration ran in rivulets down her face and neck. Her hands shook.

Jacen drew a deep breath to calm himself. So, Anja still blamed Han Solo for the death of her father, though Han denied the situation vehemently, insisting that she didn't have the correct story. But now that she had soured on Czethros, Jacen mused, perhaps she would listen to an explanation of events different from the one told by the man who had betrayed her.

Cilghal stood up. Her watery green-blue robes flowed around her. "I wish to rid my world of this illegal spice that you say is stored under the ice caps. We will go with you, Anja Gallandro, and help you destroy it. If you are telling us the truth, we will assist you in every way."

"*If* you are telling us the truth," Tenel Ka added.

"I'm not a liar," Anja said. Her entire body trembled.

"Well, you didn't exactly tell us the truth about yourself and who you worked for," Zekk pointed out. "And you *did* steal my ship."

Tenel Ka arched an eyebrow at Anja. "You also said you were not addicted to spice. This was not a fact."

"And how did you get the *Lightning Rod* on and off Kessel without any entry in the records—if you didn't lie to someone?" Jacen challenged.

Anja flushed a deep crimson. "That was different." All business now, she stood up, brushing everyone's comments aside. "Okay, I lied. But that was *before*. Things have changed, and I'm not lying

11

THE COLD, WINDING tunnels of the spice mines were almost completely devoid of light. Because glitterstim—the most common form of spice found on Kessel—was mined in total darkness, glowpanels were rarely used down here, and then only in areas where no mining was performed. Jaina shivered uncontrollably as she, Lowbacca, and Em Teedee made their way cautiously through the shafts, careful to avoid any contact with Czethros's henchmen.

Lowie's thick ginger fur provided ample protection against the cold, but Jaina's comfortable brown flightsuit warmed her only a little. Lowie was also better equipped to see in the darkness, but since no light whatsoever was allowed to filter down into the tunnels, it was difficult for either of them to discern what lay ahead.

At Lowie's suggestion, Em Teedee brightened his

optical sensors just enough to allow the two Jedi to see a meter in front of them. They did not want to attract the attention of anyone who might turn them over to Czethros. With Lowie's permission, Jaina walked a step behind, her numb fingers threaded into the fur on his back for warmth. The processed air in the tunnels chilled her throat and lungs with each breath. When she exhaled, a white mist streamed from her nostrils, further obscuring her dim vision.

A part of Jaina wished that Zekk, Jacen, and Tenel Ka were here to help them fight against the hostile takeover of Kessel. On the other hand, Jaina and Lowie were Jedi Knights themselves. They were resourceful, and she had no doubt that the two of them could find a way to seriously disrupt the plans Czethros had made.

"Do you suppose we're anywhere close to that computer terminal we need?" Jaina asked through chattering teeth.

"Yes, indeed, Mistress Jaina," Em Teedee replied in a modulated whisper. "I daresay we are now less than point-three kilometers from one of the emergency administrative terminals."

Hope warmed Jaina, but only slightly. Lowie gave a questioning bark. "Oh, yes. Quite certain," Em Teedee replied, swiveling on his microrepulsor-jets to look back at Lowie. "You see, I took the liberty of downloading not only the diagrams of the docking facilities on Kessel, but also a topographical map of all the major mining areas, along with a listing of landmarks and technical stations, before we left Master Nien Nunb's office."

"You what?" Jaina said. Lowie gave a surprised woof.

"Oh, but I assure you I had his complete authorization to—"

"We believe you, Em Teedee," Jaina said, laughing out loud with relief. "Why didn't you tell us that *before*? We could have used a more detailed map."

"Well, you didn't inquire," Em Teedee said, continuing to lead the way with his dim illumination. "The subject simply never arose. I had no idea that information would be so useful. I certainly didn't anticipate an invasion force overthrowing the legal administrators and staging a complete takeover of the spice mines."

Jaina shivered. "Neither did I. I certainly didn't dress for it."

Lowie began walking faster; knowing that they were close to their goal seemed to give him renewed energy. Jaina forced herself into a trot to keep up with the lanky Wookiee. Through the Force and her contact with her friend, Jaina could sense that a plan was beginning to form in Lowie's mind. Her spirits lifted.

"Hey, Em Teedee?"

"Yes, Mistress Jaina?"

"I'm glad you're on our team."

Lowie groaned as the terminal rejected his request for access to the secure systems on the administrative level for the third time. Jaina bit her lower lip and tried to apply some creative thinking.

"I sure wish we knew what Czethros was up to right now," she said.

Lowie shrugged and pounded a hairy fist against the terminal in frustration.

"Master Lowbacca, if I might be so bold . . . ?" Em Teedee piped up. "Perhaps my circuits can be applied to overcome some of Kessel's security routines?"

"It couldn't hurt," Jaina said.

Lowie popped open Em Teedee's casing, pulled out a few leads, and connected them to the terminal's input port. Em Teedee proceeded to "Hmmm" and "Aha" for a few minutes, then said, "Oh, yes! Most gratifying. Even better than I might have hoped."

A moment later, the image on the terminal screen split itself into five parts, with four small "windows" across the top and one large image taking up the lower two-thirds of the screen. To both Jaina and Lowie's surprise, each of the smaller images began changing rapidly, showing a different scene: the main cargo bay, various mining tunnels, the packaging chamber and conveyor belts, assorted refresher units.

Suddenly Lowie howled in triumph.

"Go back, go back!" Jaina said. In front of them appeared the image of the silver-visored Czethros seated in Nien Nunb's own administrative offices.

He was speaking to his henchmen, who were gathered around him.

"Can we get sound?" Jaina asked, her teeth chattering. Within seconds, the invasion leader's gruff voice came from the terminal speaker.

"Now that we've consolidated our position on Kessel, we need to reconfigure the main transmitter. When that is finished, we send our signal. And then nothing will be able to stop us. That signal will launch a thousand different takeovers in key industries and businesses across the galaxy. Everything perfectly timed. My army may not be large, but I have the right people in the right places. Once they take control, my network will be too powerful for even the New Republic to fight against.

"Only *I* could have brought this about." He smiled around at his confederates. "And you, my trusted colleagues, will be there to see it all happen. I've planned everything down to the last second. Nothing begins until we send our signal, because any resistance to our plan at any of the key points in my network could bring everything crashing down around us."

His fiery cyber-eye glared around at his followers as he continued. "And anyone responsible for the slightest hitch in my plan will pay with his life."

"Good work, Em Teedee." Jaina shivered as she grinned over at Lowie. "Well, we know where he is now."

Lowie rumbled thoughtfully.

"No, Master Lowbacca," Em Teedee said in a

tiny voice. "I'm afraid Master Nien Nunb did not grant me authorization to access any of the primary security systems." The translator droid gave a mechanical sigh. "Of twenty possible clearance levels, I'm afraid I've been granted only two. These levels are designated for infrastructure operations."

"And what does infrastructure operations include?" Jaina prompted.

The little droid made an embarrassed sound, as if he was clearing his throat. "The er, janitorial functions, it would seem."

Lowie's lips peeled back from his Wookiee fangs in a feral grin. Jaina's eyebrows raised, and she looked at her friend. Her imagination sparked with quite a few interesting ideas. "I think we can work with that. Don't you?"

Lowie gave a gleeful bark and began issuing orders to Em Teedee at a rapid rate as he punched in commands at the terminal. "Ah, yes. I see." Em Teedee passed the commands on through the appropriate authorization filters. "Oh my, that would be most unpleasant."

Within minutes, an alarm shrieked through the administrative levels. In the tiny image onscreen, fire-retardant systems sprang to life all around Czethros, spewing protective foam from hidden valves in the walls and ceilings. The bubbly mixture squirted across his visor and into this moss-green hair.

"Shut that thing off!" the tiny image of Czethros snapped.

Half a dozen foam-covered lackeys sprang to do his bidding. Jaina chuckled. It took several minutes for the confusion to die down and the alarms to be turned off, but Jaina and Lowie were ready.

Under Jaina's direction, Em Teedee methodically accessed each of the refresher units—and reversed the sewage containment systems. Jaina and Lowie did not have to wait long for results. In less than two minutes, Second Administrator Kymn, covered in disgusting glop, came running into the office where Czethros and his people were still cleaning up the fire-retardant mess. His eyes looked slightly wild, as if something had just happened to him that lay outside the scope of his imagination.

"Sir, we have a problem," he announced. Around him, other henchmen's noses began wrinkling in distaste. Kymn lowered his voice, leaned toward Czethros, and began whispering, his arms gesticulating to emphasize his point. Czethros grabbed the five men closest to him, rattled off a string of orders, and propelled them bodily from the room along with Administrator Kymn.

Jaina and Lowie shook with laughter. At the moment, Jaina hardly noticed the chill.

By the time Kymn and two of Czethros's mercenaries entered the maintenance turbolift, Em Teedee was ready again. The turbolift moved just a few meters before Em Teedee froze it in place with an urgent clean-and-refurbish authorization code. Despite the gravity of their situation, tears of mirth

12

ZEKK WALKED BESIDE Ambassador Cilghal as she returned to the long line of vacationers hoping to rent oceangoing vehicles. The Calamarian Jedi did not push herself forward, but waited patiently until the Yarin had finished dealing with his current customer. When the transaction was complete, the Yarin gave Cilghal a small deferential bow.

"And how may I make your stay at Crystal Reef more enjoyable?" the treelike creature asked ponderously, reaching for Cilghal's flippered hand. The Jedi ambassador accepted the question graciously. At the corner of his vision, Zekk saw Anja roll her eyes; she'd been through this tedious routine herself.

With her free hand, Cilghal gestured to Jacen. "Please allow me to introduce Jacen Solo . . . son of the New Republic Chief of State. I'm guiding him as a special favor to his uncle . . . Master Luke Skywalker."

Zekk noticed an instant change of expression on the Yarin's woody face. "And these are his friends, Tenel Ka—princess of the Hapes system—as well as Anja and Zekk. They are all from the Jedi academy," Cilghal continued. "Naturally, I take my duties as special ambassador for Mon Calamari seriously, and I'm afraid my young friend here, Jacen Solo, has his heart set on showing his friends the beauties of the Calamarian oceans."

Zekk admired the older Jedi's melodious voice as she spoke soothingly, persuasively to the Yarin. "I'm sure you can understand how important this could be for the public image of Crystal Reef: Jedi extolling the virtues and beauties of our resorts, the gratitude of the Royal House of Hapes . . . perhaps even a visit from Han Solo and Chief of State Leia Organa Solo herself."

As if blown by a light breeze, the Yarin began to sway back and forth to the singsong rhythm of Cilghal's words. "Hmmm. Ah yes, I see. Unfortunately, I have no submersibles left for rent." At Cilghal's expression of disappointment, he hurried on. "But if you would allow me, Ambassador, being harbormaster at Crystal Reef does have its privileges. I have my own private submersible nearby. I use it mainly for fixing small underwater problems, and for a bit of pottering about, but I would be honored if you would consent to it. It may be a tight fit for five people, but I'm sure—"

"Hey, that's great!" Jacen said. "It'll do just fine."

"Why, thank you. We'd be delighted," Cilghal assured the tree creature.

The Yarin beamed at the small group. His kindly eyes lit on Anja. "I'm sorry, young lady, that I almost disappointed you. You should have let me know you were in such distinguished company."

Zekk saw Anja blink, as if surprised that the Yarin now believed her to be in "distinguished company." Her cheeks reddened, as if it had not occurred to her until now that running around with Jedi Knights, royalty, ambassadors, and the children of war heroes and the Chief of State might actually impress some people.

"This way, this way," the Yarin said, motioning them toward his private dock. He gave Zekk a shrewd glance. "And you, young Jedi, have the look of a fine pilot about you, if I'm not mistaken. I believe I could entrust my minisubmersible to your capable hands." Zekk looked at the Yarin in surprise.

"Hey, I'm a pretty fine pilot myself," Anja objected as they reached the dock where the minisub was tethered.

"Zekk is an excellent choice," Tenel Ka interrupted. "I believe he is the finest pilot among us."

"Besides," Zekk muttered to Anja, "you're not going to pilot anything until I get *my* ship back." She clamped her lips shut and folded her arms across her chest. "I'm sure Cilghal will help me pilot the sub, since I'm in unfamiliar waters."

The treelike harbormaster opened the hatch with

one branchy hand and helped the young Jedi climb down into the submersible. "And you, Ambassador," the Yarin said as he helped Cilghal down, "are probably most familiar with Calamarian ocean-going craft. I trust you will be able to handle any emergencies that might arise?"

Cilghal gave him a stately nod.

"We'll take good care of your little sub," Zekk assured him. "Does it have a name?"

The Yarin gave a wheeze that Zekk figured must have been a chuckle and said, "I call her the *Elfa*. Among my people, it is a word that means fish-so-small-that-it-is-not-worth-catching."

"We can't thank you enough, Harbormaster," Cilghal said. "We will take good care of your *Elfa*."

The ocean beneath the arctic ice was beautiful. The blue-green glow of water-filtered daylight transformed every creature, sea plant, or chunk of ice into a thing of magic. Particulates suspended in the water sparkled like gold dust. The *Elfa* was smaller by far than the *Lightning Rod*, and less maneuverable because it was in water, but Zekk enjoyed every moment of piloting it.

"The transponder signal's getting stronger," Anja announced in a ragged voice. "We're almost to the spice stash." Her breath seemed labored. Zekk wondered if she had a fear of enclosed places and disliked the unusual feeling of being deep under water. Either that, he decided, or she was going through spice withdrawal again.

"Just let me know if I need to make any course adjustments," Zekk said.

Over the past two hours, Cilghal had shown him how to use most of the systems on the tiny submersible, and he now felt as comfortable with the *Elfa* as he had ever felt with any ship besides the *Lightning Rod*.

"Over there. Is that it?" Jacen asked, pointing.

"I believe so. You have excellent eyes," Tenel Ka said.

"Thanks. You have pretty nice eyes, too," Jacen teased.

"The signal's strong and clear," Anja said, ignoring the banter. "Do you see it?"

"Got it," Zekk said, already making the course correction.

In less than five minutes he had maneuvered them into position beside the cache, which had been tucked away beneath blocks of free-floating arctic ice. The four separate containers were sealed, armored cases, quickly stashed there for safekeeping, anchored to the ice.

Anja crowded close to the windowport, looking over Zekk's shoulder to get a better view. Her face was flushed, her breathing ragged, her hair damp with perspiration.

"Okay, now what?" Zekk asked.

"Now we destroy them, just as we all agreed," Anja said.

"Hey, I hate to mention this, but those containers

look like they're pretty well armored. How do you expect to get rid of them?"

"I believe I can be of assistance there," Cilghal said. She set to work at the controls of the two grappling arms attached to the minisub, maneuvering until one of the sealed containers was in her grasp. Then she squeezed with the claw mechanism until one of the claws pierced the armor and the buoyant container began to fill with water.

"Should we just let it sink?" Zekk asked.

"No, that's not good enough!" Anja snapped. She calmed herself and lowered her voice. "Czethros's people would still be able to locate it by the transponder and retrieve the spice. This is valuable stuff, remember."

"In that case, perhaps this will work," Cilghal said, reaching out with the other claw-arm to grasp a second heavy cargo container. She swung them both outward and then back together again to smash them into each other. The already-punctured storage bin burst at the impact and a flood of tiny sealed ampoules cascaded from the container. Some of the vials shattered; others just drifted free and then slowly began to sink into the frigid depths of the ocean.

"Is this an acceptable solution?" Tenel Ka asked Anja.

Anja was silent for a full minute, just staring at the shimmering ampoules in the water around them and panting. Zekk wondered if she regretted her decision to destroy them, but a moment later Anja answered.

She raised a triumphant fist. "Yesss!" She gave a weak laugh. "Even if Czethros's men manage to find the transponder signal now, I'd like to see them all searching several square kilometers of ocean floor and trying to collect all of those tiny little ampoules—one by one."

Zekk gave a satisfied nod. "As Jaina would say, what are we waiting for? Let's smash the other ones."

Still leaning over his shoulder, Anja whispered, "Two down, two to go."

While Zekk handled the minisub's piloting controls, Cilghal deftly maneuvered the pincer claws, grasping the final sealed container of andris spice with one of them. To Jacen's surprise, the Jedi ambassador stopped and blinked her huge fishy eyes. "Something is not right."

The submersible's lights seemed to have attracted something in the murky, ice-clogged water . . . something large and dangerous and seeking prey.

"What's that?" Jacen leaned toward a thick transparisteel porthole. "There's a shadow out there, something . . . swimming." He let his eyes fall halfway closed, reached out with the Force. "Uh-oh."

As he stood, stretching his thoughts into the dark water, a giant yellow eye flashed in front of the window, its pupil as large as Jacen's head. His eyelids snapped up, and for a fraction of a second, he froze, pinned by its cold and angry gaze.

"Jacen, my friend, do you have a 'bad feeling' about this?" Tenel Ka asked.

He nodded. The creature swam forward. Its eye was followed by a mouth filled with huge fangs, each one seemingly large enough to crush an X-wing starfighter.

"Look out!" Jacen cried.

Zekk and the Calamarian ambassador grappled with the sub's controls. The minisub rocked back and forth under the water as the startled sea beast moved closer to look at the curious thing.

A huge tentacle the size of a space-station docking tether whipped across their front field of view, slithering, probing.

Though the creature felt hungry to Jacen, it remained cautious as it approached its new victim. The minisub turned about, its propellers whirring in the water, pushing them ever so slowly toward safety.

The giant sea creature swam past again like an immense underwater ship, not attacking yet. Its scaly hide rippled as it cruised by. More tentacles streamed out in all directions.

Jacen gave a low whistle. "It's awfully big. Do you know what it is, Cilghal?"

The Mon Calamarian shook her large head. "There are many things deep in the oceans of my world that have never been named, or even seen, by living creatures."

"We might not qualify as living creatures for long, if that thing decides to go for us," Anja said.

The current from the beast's passage stirred the waters, making the minisub buck and sway. Zekk grasped the controls more tightly. Jacen pressed his face against the cold porthole, observing the armored hide, the long neck, the huge head with its mouth that could swallow the largest of fish. And tentacles everywhere.

A thick, sinuous arm struck the side of the minisub. Not hard—just an exploratory tap—but it sent them careening end over end beneath the water. Bubbles burst out all around the submersible.

Cilghal wrestled with the controls. "Hang on," she said as Zekk tried to steady the craft in the midst of the foamy turmoil.

Anja was thrown backward into her seat.

Lights flickered and dimmed inside the cabin before the emergency generators kicked on, adding fresh illumination.

Zekk grunted as his head smacked against the wall. "Tell me this sub has some sort of defense system."

"Unfortunately, this is not a fact," Tenel Ka said. "And I doubt we are capable of outswimming that creature."

Jacen looked through the front windowports into the cold arctic sea. He sensed that the giant shadowy hulk would turn and swim back, return for another pass—and that this time it would be less reticent to make a full-fledged assault. He reached out with his mind, trying to use the Force to find the massive creature's primitive mind. But the beast's attention was entirely absorbed by the new prey.

"That wasn't even an attack yet," Zekk said. "The thing was just checking us out." He rubbed the back of his neck, as if he tingled, and looked back at Jacen. "Next time it'll want a meal."

The minisub's stabbing lights spread out in white cones through the water. Bubbles still drifted up, shrouding them in a watery bead curtain. Moments later the gigantic silhouette swam into the light, showing off its thick body core studded with long deadly tentacles, and its large ravenous mouth. The creature undulated toward them, thrashing through the water. The tiny underwater vehicle would never be able to travel that fast. They could not escape through sheer energy alone.

The creature's maw opened wide.

Cilghal added power to the hull attitude jets, tilting the craft at a steep angle to rise toward the jagged ceiling of ice under the polar cap. The sub sputtered out of the way. Snapping with its tentacles, the monster pursued.

Despite Cilghal's attempts to control it during the violent evasive maneuvers, the small grappling claw that held the last andris container ripped loose. The second claw bent and jammed. The crate popped free, drifting . . . slowly sinking.

"There goes the spice!" Anja said, and Jacen couldn't be sure if she was disappointed or just observing a fact.

Seeing the bright morsel fall away from the larger craft, the sea monster swerved and ducked toward it. Long tentacles reached out, grasped, and in a single swift movement the creature's fanged mouth came forward and chomped down on the container. Swordlike teeth tore through the outer coverings, freeing the spice ampoules.

Vials began to shatter . . . and the beast swallowed a thousand doses of andris. All at once.

Jacen stared as the monster gulped down an immeasurable quantity of the intense stimulant. "Uh-oh," he said, "now we're really in trouble. If you thought that monster was hyper before, wait until the andris kicks in."

Below them, the creature thrashed about in growing agitation. And then it turned its attention back to the minisub.

13

UNDER THE HUMID, hazy sunlight of Yavin 4, a steady flow of Jedi Knights came and learned and became the hope of the galaxy. Nothing would stop them now.

Master Luke Skywalker considered his students over the years, remembering them all. Alone at first, he had been so tentative, so uncertain, as he tried to bring back the association of heroic fighters who had performed so many legendary deeds in the days of the Old Republic.

But now the Jedi training center had taken on a life of its own. The new Jedi learned as much from each other, and from his former students, as they took from Luke's lectures and intensive training sessions. Never again would the order of Jedi Knights be limited by the bottleneck of having only one teacher and a single student.

Luke's very first trainees, the batch of twelve he

had taken and trained after his Jedi search, were full Jedi Knights. They traveled throughout the young New Republic fighting battles, helping to maintain planetary stability, and performing the various good works a Jedi was called upon to do. Some of those candidates had become legends in their own right, a new generation. Now, with the remarkable capabilities of Han and Leia's twins, as well as their young Jedi friends and their younger brother Anakin, Luke felt that the Force had truly been reborn. The Jedi Knights were strong now. He did not believe they would ever fall again.

He wished Obi-Wan Kenobi could be here to see him now. The "old wizard" from the Jundland Wastes had changed his life more profoundly than Luke could ever have imagined. Kenobi had turned a simple farm boy from a desert planet into a Jedi. And, in so doing, he had single-handedly set in motion the events that had brought down the Empire, restored the Jedi Knights, and helped create the benevolent New Republic. Kenobi had died sacrificing himself on the Death Star before he could see any of his seeds bear fruit, but Luke would never forget him. The teachings of the old Jedi would always be a part of Luke's continuing work at the Jedi academy.

Students came and went here on Yavin 4. Luke's partner in teaching, Tionne, had been one of his first students. In order to keep from repeating the mistakes of the past, she made certain the candidates were well grounded in history. Tionne loved to tell tales of past Jedi. She shared her knowledge of the lore of those who fought for the light side of the Force in ancient times. Through her teachings, the legends survived and grew, fixed again in history—though the evil Emperor had tried to obliterate them from the memory of all living beings.

As Luke stood pondering, Artoo trundled up, bleeping a greeting and chittering a new assessment of supplies and needed equipment. Luke rested a hand on the astromech droid's domed head.

"Relax, Artoo. I was just thinking about how things have changed."

He recalled his uncle Owen and aunt Beru, who had tried to shield him from all traumas his life would bring. Their attempts to corral him on a desert world and keep his dreams small had been unsuccessful. His aunt and uncle had wanted him to hide on Tatooine, to live the uneventful life of a quiet, simple moisture farmer. Uncle Owen had known Luke's heritage, who his father was, and what dark connections a Skywalker child might have. Despite the best of intentions, the overprotectiveness of Owen and Beru Lars had nearly cost Luke—and the galaxy—the ultimate freedom.

Visions of the last time he had been home as a boy filled his mind—the burned-out moisture farm, the blackened corpses of Uncle Owen and Aunt Beru, gunned down by stormtroopers in an act of terrorism. He had no idea what horrors they had experienced in their last moments, whether his aunt and uncle had been tortured by the Imperials for information . . . even though they'd had nothing to tell.

But the stormtroopers had killed them anyway.

He wished Uncle Owen and Aunt Beru could be here now to witness all he had accomplished. Luke Skywalker had established a firm place in history. But lasting victories often demanded harsh sacrifice.

Luke vowed that such violent repression would never happen again, not if he or his Jedi Knights could prevent it. There would be battles to fight, and there would be casualties. He didn't try to give his new trainees a false sense of reality. There were great costs associated with being a Jedi. They might be called on to suffer, to feel pain . . . or to die for a cause.

But Jedi did what they believed was right—not what was simple or safe. They trusted the Force.

In front of the rebuilt temple on the training field, a dozen students sparred and clashed. Some practiced alone, using their minds to work with the Force. Others developed the fine points of teamwork. His students, all of them . . . but they were also their own people. They would go through their own ordeals.

Despite the perils he knew some of his students would eventually face—and that the young Jedi Knights might be facing even now on their quest to find Anja out in the galaxy—Luke had no regrets. He had made difficult choices. He had done what he'd had to do. His students were doing the same.

And the Force was with them all.

14

GIVEN THE UNDERSEA monster's enormous body mass, the powerful spice worked more quickly than Zekk could possibly have imagined. He gripped the controls and tried to maneuver the minisub away with all possible speed, but they gained only a minimal distance—nowhere near enough.

After swallowing the prodigious amount of andris, the beast flailed briefly, then began darting from left to right, its tentacles thrashing, grabbing, jittering, as if from seizures and convulsions.

Jacen rubbed his temples, concentrating, then gave a sigh of exasperation. "There's no way I can get through to it now. It's got a storm going through its brain!"

Cilghal released the useless grasper controls of the sub's remaining mechanical claw and threw herself into helping Zekk. He pushed the minisub's engines beyond their maximum recommended levels, heading higher into the inverted canyons of iceberg roots, toward the blocky mass of the polar cap and away from the thrashing beast.

"Maybe he won't notice us," Zekk muttered.

"Yeah, and maybe Han Solo's on his way to rescue us at this very moment," Anja said with clear scorn. Her face was flushed, her forehead sweating—but she seemed to be fighting internal battles beyond simple fear for their survival. "Face it, Zekk—we're in trouble."

The leviathan's flailings became even more frenzied. It spun about, tentacles waving like handfuls of bullwhips. Finally, it focused its energy on a single target: the minisub. The creature turned its long head on its sinuous neck, its glowing yellow eyes flaring with a brighter light as the monster dove in to attack.

Cilghal uttered a wordless sound as she jammed the throttles from the copilot's station. Zekk let her maneuver, since she was more familiar with ocean-going vessels. The sub's propellers and bubbles swirled behind its main body as they shot off through the frigid water.

The sea monster followed, reaching forward, stretching, trying to grasp. The tip of one tentacle brushed against the main propeller on the rear of the sub, which sheared it off. The creature drew back, but seconds later the maddened monster resumed the chase, frothing the water behind it. Its sharp silver-fanged jaws clacked together, as if prepared to cut through the metal hull.

With a rapid sideways motion, a tentacle slammed into the directional fin that guarded one engine. The inner compartment of the minisub rang like a heavy bell from the blow. The engines squealed and groaned, spilling smoke, but they continued to work—just barely.

Zekk and Cilghal took the sub higher, closer to the ice-locked surface. Zekk's ears popped with the pressure difference.

Outside, drifting slabs of ice smashed against the hull with loud thunks and bangs that reverberated through the chamber. Cilghal swerved the minisub's rudder, and Zekk tilted the craft to avoid a knotted underwater cliff that dangled beneath a heavy ice-berg.

By grasping the rough ice with its tentacles, the sea creature hauled itself forward. Closer and closer.

"Up there!" Zekk said, pointing to a fissure in the ice. "It's too small for the creature to follow us inside." Cilghal saw and nodded.

Anja frowned, covering her fear with her usual show of skepticism. She seemed to be exceedingly tense and appeared to be shivering. "I doubt even the sub could get in there."

The creature lashed out with its sharp-ended tentacles and slapped the ice. Large blue-white chunks broke off and drifted around them, like boulders rising and falling in slow motion. The minisub ducked below a jagged ceiling of frozen ice and accelerated as the gap widened, spewing bubbles. The sea creature charged after them, thrashing, groping with its tentacles. One of the long whiplike appendages finally fastened on to the rear of the sub, somehow gaining purchase with its suckers on the smooth hull.

Inside, Jacen was tossed into Anja. Her breathing rasped in his ears. Tenel Ka was the only one who managed to keep her place. Zekk was thrown half-way from the pilot's seat to slam against the sub wall. Cilghal gripped the controls and held herself erect.

"It's got us," Zekk cried, trying to regain his balance. His ears ringing, he pushed himself back into his seat. Cilghal throttled the engines down, let the minisub drift backward for a second, and then revved up the engines in a sudden burst to push them forward again. Slowly, the slippery hull pulled free from the suction cups, leaving the monster's bruised and throbbing tentacle behind.

Bubbles sprayed in front of the windowports, and Cilghal could barely see to help Zekk navigate. Huge, jagged chunks of ice blocked their way. One smashed into the front of the sub, making a scar on the thick windowport and shearing off the minisub's remaining grappling arm.

Cilghal placed a flippered hand on Zekk's arm. He felt strength flow into his mind. Guided by the Force, Zekk twisted the rudder from left to right, and the sub looped around an obstacle, more because of the Force than from any spectacular piloting skill. The torn end of the ruined grappling arm sparked and sprayed, then went dead as Zekk disabled its power systems.

"You're sure there aren't any weapons on this thing?" Jacen called from the rear of the sub. "Anything at all?"

"It's a working craft, mainly for tourists or that Yarin's personal use," Cilghal answered. "I'm sure it was never meant to drive off an attack."

"There is the towing beam." Tenel Ka pointed out a small tractor-beam that could fasten onto an underwater object and drag it to the surface. "Perhaps that could assist us."

"Hey!" Jacen said. "Good idea."

"Great," Anja said with a snort. "Am I the only sane person down here? Or does someone else agree that the last thing we want is to pull that monster *closer* to us!" Perspiration stood out on her upper lip.

"Not that—we can grab a big chunk of ice and pull it behind us. Block the way," Zekk said, seeing Tenel Ka's idea.

Cilghal didn't argue, immediately running her webbed hands across the controls. A pulsing beam stabbed out from the rear of the sub and grasped a knob of ice, yanking the berg into the path behind them. The ice moved slowly through the thick, cold water—but it did move. The frozen wall drifted enough to cover their escape.

The creature rammed into it, wrapping tentacles around jagged blue-white edges.

The moving iceberg pounded into others, slamming ice against rock-hard ice. Zekk moved the minisub up into the fissure between the broken chunks of the polar cap, rising higher. Cilghal continued to use what was left of the ice chunk as a shield. Shattered pieces of other floating mountains snapped off and drifted back into the channel through which they had just passed.

The sea monster suddenly found itself surrounded by a hail of floating boulders. Its tentacles reached out to knock the ice chunks aside as the beast struggled forward in pursuit of its prey. But the icebergs ground together, sealing off access.

The discouraged monster battered its tentacles against the ice. At last, expelling a mouthful of bubbles and gnashing its long silvery teeth, the creature swam away, still writhing with energy. Jacen sensed the monster propelling itself into the dark depths of the polar ocean in search of easier prey. The overdose of spice would give it energy to hunt for a long, long time. . . .

Zekk had difficulty maneuvering toward the surface. Ice walls closed around them, sealing off their retreat while blocking any forward motion. The sub couldn't even rise up to where the occupants could reach the cold air on the surface.

Jacen and Tenel Ka stared in the direction of the departed monster as more ice chunks lodged into place further sealing them off.

"The beast believes it has given us a mortal wound," Tenel Ka said. "It has gone to hunt elsewhere."

"Practically speaking," Zekk said, "we *do* have a mortal wound. Is it as bad as I think it is, Cilghal?"

The Calamarian ambassador examined the controls, worked them a bit, but the minisub made no headway. The engines rumbled and smoked. "Our vehicle is damaged," she said. "Our air is limited, and we find ourselves trapped in a maze of blue ice."

Zekk grunted in acknowledgment. He hadn't wanted to be right about the damage to the sub.

"At least we got away from that monster," Jacen said, always the optimist.

"Great," Anja answered in a shaky voice. She looked very much on edge, very distressed. "But have you noticed that we're stranded beneath the polar ice cap?"

15

HUDDLED IN THE wall channel of a dormant atmosphere factory, Jaina and Lowie set about determining the best way to fight Black Sun's invasion force.

The rock walls all around them were cold, and the air was thin—but the environment would be far worse if they traveled up the long-rusted stairs to reach the open surface.

No matter how harsh the conditions they faced, though, Jaina knew they had to do something, *any-thing* to prevent Czethros from enacting his terrible schemes. The New Republic depended on them.

Lowie looked out of the tunnel entrance into the shadows of the broad pit that rose vertically toward the surface. In the past, the miners on Kessel had constructed gigantic factories to chemically release gases frozen in the rocks and spew them upward to thicken the atmosphere. But such extravagant efforts had been only a temporary solution, and in recent years the small planet had rapidly reverted to its natural state of frigid cold with a rarefied atmosphere.

Next to the rock wall, the Wookiee took a deep breath. Fine threads of frost laced his ginger fur, and the lanky young Jedi looked miserable—but a fire of determination burned in his golden eyes. He growled.

Jania understood much of the Wookiee language, but Em Teedee translated anyway. "Master Lowbacca suggests that our primary mission should be to cause a serious malfunction to the sophisticated transmitter Czethros intends to use."

"Agreed," Jaina said, looking at Lowie. "If we get rid of that transmitter, Czethros can't send his signal. His coordinated plan fails."

"Yes, but Mistress Jaina," Em Teedee chimed in, "however are we to disable such a large piece of equipment?"

Jaina shrugged and then smiled at the shiny little translating droid. "First thing is to find some sort of explosives. . . . Then we may just need *you* to sneak in there, Em Teedee."

The floating little droid's electronic squawk reverberated through the tunnels.

Each of the control rooms in the spice mine catacombs was sealed with a heavy door, code-locked and computer-controlled. Lowie used his programming expertise, with an occasional assist from the little droid, to crack the codes and force their way into one of the equipment lockers.

It wasn't difficult to find a supply of shaped explosives of the sort used for blasting mine tunnels. Kessel was, after all, an industrial excavation area. Lowie found small packaged cylinders marked with red HAZARD labels. He hefted them in his hands and looked over at Em Teedee's microrepulsorjets. He gave a growl of satisfaction.

"You can handle these, Em Teedee," Jaina said. "They don't weigh much."

"Oh, my!" the little droid replied. "But I've never carried explosives before."

"Not much different from a rock," Jaina said encouragingly, "except that these'll explode if you bump against anything."

"I appreciate your support, Mistress Jaina, but I find your optimism . . . unsettling." She patted the floating silvery ovoid as it hovered in the air.

The tunnels were empty. The spice mine loading docks were shut down, denying access to any cargo ships, since Black Sun had taken over. Czethros could not keep up this charade for long, but security threats against Kessel oftentimes required such random crackdowns, and the merchants waiting in orbit would just have to wait longer. No complaints or unusual-occurrence reports would be filed for at least another standard day.

Czethros would no doubt launch his widespread takeover before then. Therefore, Jaina and her friends needed to complete their sabotage before that could happen.

Most of the dusty tunnels were silent and abandoned. The actual numbers in the Black Sun occupation fleet were quite small, but they had placed armed guards in key positions. Nien Nunb and his loyal followers had been sealed in the slave barracks left over from the days when Kessel had been a prison facility. Many other workers, along with a few unfortunate cargo ship pilots, were being kept under guard behind force fields. It was an unstable situation, and Jaina knew it wouldn't take much to turn the tables.

But first, they had to get rid of that transmitter.

They climbed up through air shafts, avoiding lift platforms for fear of whom they might encounter. Finally, they reached the upper main loading dock on the surface. Access doors would be closed but not locked. No one in their right mind would go for a casual walk on the surface of Kessel.

According to maps and diagrams of the spice mine and its comm station, they had a good idea where Kessel's sophisticated transmitter— currently being modified by Black Sun—must be located. The powerful antenna was large . . . and probably well guarded. Two human-sized intruders could not possibly remain hidden as they made their way across the bleak, rugged surface.

But a small silvery droid might just be able to slip in undetected. . . .

The ships in the cargo bay sat quiet and empty, as

if the place was abandoned. Jaina recognized one of the familiar craft, though. A small man worked furtively beneath the engines.

"Lilmit's still around!" Jaina said. While the other pilots were taken prisoner, Lilmit had probably been allowed to remain here because he worked for Black Sun.

The strange man looked up, and his eyes went wide as he noticed the Wookiee and the young woman. The hapless smuggler raised his webbed hands in panic. "Oh, no! But you're *gone*. Your ship left. I saw the docking records. Go away—there's nothing more I can tell you."

"Great," Jaina muttered. "Now we'll have to take *him* hostage."

Lilmit wailed. "Please, I didn't have anything to do with this. I just wanted to get off Kessel before the Black Sun takeover. Czethros will be furious if he sees that I'm still here."

Jaina looked at Lowie, wondering how they would ever manage to keep Lilmit quiet. If the little man caused a scene and got them noticed, they were sunk. But instead, the frantic smuggler ran into his ship to hide and sealed the hatch.

"I do believe our diminutive friend has panicked," Em Teedee said.

"Let's hope he stays quiet for just a little while," Jaina said.

Lowie growled and gestured toward the outer doors of the cargo bay. If they could complete their mission quickly and hide again in the tunnels, they wouldn't be found, no matter what Lilmit did. Jaina suspected that the terrified smuggler would not want to call anyone's attention to his presence. But then again, the little pilot's fear of Czethros might just prompt him to report the presence of two unauthorized young Jedi. . . .

Lowie chuffed something again, and the translating droid replied, "Indeed, Master Lowbacca, 'What *are* we waiting for?' "

Together, Jaina and Lowie reached the door, grabbed a pair of breath masks from a locker, and slapped them over their faces. The slow trickle of oxygen would be enough to keep them alive in the harsh environment, though the freezing temperatures and the crackling dry air would take its toll before long. They didn't have much time.

Jaina unsealed the hatch, and they passed through. Gusts of wind roared after them as air flowed out of the pressurized cargo bay. They stood out on the bleak, white alkaline desert of Kessel's surface.

"Lovely place," Jaina said, her voice muffled by the breath mask.

Frost clung to the rocks, and steam rose into the air from heating and recirculation vents deep in the spice mines. Near the foreshortened horizon they saw the metal and wire-mesh flower of the massive transmitter. Czethros would use it to send his coded, high-powered signal burst announcing that now was the time for Black Sun's ultimate takeover.

The flat, broken land was strewn with boulders and chunks of powdery white salt dried into lumps and low pillars. Cracks split the landscape. Jaina saw very few places for them to hide; her jumpsuit, along with Lowie's ginger-brown fur, would stand out like a striking beacon.

They had no choice but to send Em Teedee.

His fingers already numb with cold, Lowie bent down to manipulate the tiny cords. Using a special quick-release knot, he attached the two canisters of explosives below the hovering droid's casing. With her hands, Jaina showed Em Teedee the distance he needed to keep between his casing and the rough surface of the planetoid.

"You have this much play between the explosive and the ground right now," she said. "We'll need you to fly as low as possible to keep from being seen, but *don't* let the explosives hit a rock."

"Indeed, Mistress Jaina. I assure you that I won't."

Lowie grunted something, and Em Teedee snapped, "What do you mean by 'famous last words'? I intend to follow our plan exactly!"

Lowie touched the buttons on the shaped charges with his claws and chattered to the droid.

Em Teedee answered in alarm, "Six standard minutes? Do you think that will be sufficient time?" The Wookiee shrugged.

"These aren't high-capacity charges, Em Teedee," Jaina said. "I don't think they're made with long timers."

"Very well, I shall do my best." The little droid hovered off the ground and then, with a burst of his microrepulsorjets, skimmed across the powdery surface of Kessel like a glinting silver bullet. Keeping low, he wove around rocks, over fissures, across the broken and rugged terrain.

A troop of guards would likely be stationed in a protective hut near the transmitter, just waiting for Czethros to send his signal. The droid had to get there before they saw him.

Em Teedee increased speed, still painfully aware that he could not allow the canisters of explosives to strike against a hard rock or a projection of encrusted salt. His internal clock counted down the seconds that remained on the bomb timers. The transmitting dish seemed very far away.

Em Teedee pushed his microjets faster and faster, drawing closer. Finally, the structure loomed up ahead of him: scooped amplifiers and curved screens to focus the communication beam. The miniaturized droid rose like a tiny satellite over the lip, then dropped toward the center of the flower. There, an aiming antenna would direct the signal while the pulse ricocheted off the parabolic petals and increased its power, sending it out to all secret receiving stations attuned to the Black Sun's command frequency.

After he landed in the center, Em Teedee gently touched the explosive canisters to the central control point, jerked upward against the quick-release knots to detach the short cables, then rose into the air. He had very little time left, and he was anxious to get away. Stealth had required him to take longer than anticipated reaching the station, and now that there was nothing to delay him, the droid shot upward and sped away.

He must have made a fine glittering target, because two guards barreled out of a small hutment beside the transmitting station. They were curious at first, gazing up at him, then began shouting. One of the men turned back to the transmitting station as if he realized something must be wrong. The other guard grabbed for his weapon, but didn't seem to know what to shoot at.

Em Teedee streaked across the rocky landscape and vanished into the distance.

Jaina and Lowie stood up, waving him on toward the doorway that would lead back into the pressurized docking bay.

When the translating droid was only a hundred meters away from them, the transmitter erupted in a blossom of orange fire. Shrapnel blew sky-high— some of it perhaps even into orbit, because of Kessel's low gravity.

Jaina and Lowie watched as the fires from the explosion slowly sputtered out for lack of oxygen. Huge sections of the antenna fell, teetering before they collapsed. A few seconds later, the shock wave and the sound reached them at the docking bay doors, high-pitched and tinny due to the thin air.

"Let's go!" Jaina said. "They're really going to be after us now."

They ducked back inside the spice mines of Kessel, hoping they could find a safe place to hide.

•   •   •

When Czethros learned of the disaster, his roar of rage was almost as loud as the explosion itself. His blazing cyber-eye scanned back and forth, looking for someone to blame.

"Timing is everything!" he bellowed. "If I don't send my signal, the uprising will never commence—and unless we do this all at once, the New Republic will find a way to crush each separate little brush-fire."

A guard nodded. "I understand, my Lord Czethros."

"Of course you understand! An *idiot* could understand. But what can you do about it?"

"Nothing that I know of, my Lord Czethros."

The Black Sun lieutenant stormed back and forth in Nien Nunb's office, which he had commandeered. He knew his superiors were counting on him, and he knew that the leaders of Black Sun were not very forgiving when something went wrong.

"I thought you had imprisoned everyone who could cause problems for us," Czethros said, whirling about. "What did you forget to take into account? Who is still missing?"

"I don't know, my Lord Czethros."

"Of course you don't know, or the situation would already be under control!" He pounded a hand on the Chief Administrator's low tabletop. He wished the Sullustan were taller so that his office and its furnishings would have been a bit more comfortable for a man of his size.

Czethros glared at the guard. The other armed mercenaries milling about in the hall nervously awaited their turn for a reprimand. Each hoped he would survive the wrath of Czethros.

"It's safe to say we have some sort of little rodents unaccounted for. The saboteurs know what they're doing, and they intend to ruin my plans. Make sure all our prisoners are securely locked away. Then I want full teams to comb every inch of the spice mines. We must find whoever is responsible for blowing up my transmitting station. I want them—dead or alive. I don't care which."

He turned, not deigning even to look at his crew anymore, then slowly glanced back over his shoulder. "Of course, if you don't find them for me to torture"—his cracked lips curled in a faint smile— "I'll be forced to take out my frustrations on some of you instead."

16

ANJA HAD NEVER felt so out of control.

While the Jedi all around her in the minisub worked with brisk determination to diagnose and fix the ailments of the *Elfa*, she felt herself slipping away into a zone of pain somewhere between madness and death.

Her vision narrowed and filled with static at the edges. She found she could not concentrate on what her friends were doing—the need for spice was too great, no matter how she tried to push it back. The tiny claustrophobic vessel felt unbearably hot, stifling, despite their arctic prison. Unreasonable quantities of perspiration soaked her leather headband, streamed into her large eyes, ran down her neck and back to leave damp stains on her clothing.

The others around her were talking, planning, brainstorming, but it all seemed so far away. A deep ache burned in her muscles and ate its way down to her bones, igniting liquid agony in every joint of her body. Moving her hands or any part of her body produced an instant punishing pain. So she did not move. Each breath became a struggle. Her head throbbed with unimaginable pressure. She realized now that only one substance in the galaxy could put an end to her agony: andris.

Stupid, her mind raged. How could she have let this happen to her? Addiction was for fools and weaklings, not for someone like herself—independent, intelligent, strong-willed. She had never meant for the andris to affect her this way. She'd always thought she was in charge of her own body, but now she was a prisoner of spice.

Fool! she snarled at herself. Anja had been sure that addiction was for other people, weak people. She had convinced herself from the beginning that she would be able to handle it. She'd known when she started taking spice that many people had been destroyed by addiction. Anja had watched it, had known it for a fact. And yet, with firm conviction, she had believed that it would not happen to her.

I am strong. Immune. Invincible.

Anja gave a bitter laugh. *Delirious* was more like it. Somewhere in the back of Anja's mind, a memory stirred, a childhood memory of her mother shaking her head and saying, "So like your father. Taking the easy way even though it's dangerous, and not thinking for a moment that you could be hurt." Anja could not have been older than three or

four when her mother had said those words. Her
mother had died while Anja was still young. Yet
somehow part of Anja's feverish brain had remembered. She didn't even try to control her shuddering.

So—she and her father had something in common: both took foolish risks, both believed themselves indestructible. Anja drew a ragged breath.
She had to admit now that Han Solo was probably
telling the truth. In the end, it had most likely been
her father's foolishness that had killed him—just as
her own foolishness would kill her now.

She gripped the arms of her seat as streamers of
fire unfurled in her muscles and joints. Short of
dying, there was only one way to stop the pain.

"Spice!" she rasped.

The frenetic activity around her quieted and, as if
from a distance, she heard Jacen's voice say, "Anja?
Are you all right?"

"Spice," she repeated. "Andris."

"It's fine. We managed to destroy almost everything."

Something—a hand?—touched her arm, and
where it touched, her suffering was more bearable.
She blinked hard, trying to focus her vision.

Jacen's face, complete with lopsided grin, swam
into view. "Hey, you look terrible."

"That's because . . . I'm dying," she managed
in a hoarse whisper.

Anger flashed in his brandy-brown eyes. "No
you're not!"

Tenel Ka's serious face suddenly appeared beside

Jacen's. The warrior girl stretched out her single hand and made a brief, thorough check of Anja's pulse, skin temperature, pupil dilation, and muscular tremors. At each place the warrior girl's fingers touched, the pain eased—just for a moment—before she moved on.

"You will not die, Anja Gallandro," she said. "We will not allow it."

Anja suddenly felt the relief of another Jedi touch on her left hand. A pair of emerald-green eyes stared into hers. "It's bad, isn't it?" Zekk asked. "Spice withdrawal, right?"

Anja felt too weak to reply, but Zekk seemed to see the answer in her eyes. "I went through something similar. Well, not with drugs. I was addicted to using the dark side of the Force. I knew it was wrong, but I told myself I had good reasons for what I was doing. Anyway, when I wanted to stop, the dark side didn't want to let me go. I almost didn't make it." He glanced up briefly at Jacen and Tenel Ka. "If it hadn't been for my friends, I don't think I would have."

Anja shivered. Her teeth rattled together. Tenel Ka reached out and pushed a few sweaty strands of hair out of Anja's eyes. Cool, tingling relief followed her friend's touch.

Her *friends*, Anja thought with distant surprise: Tenel Ka, Jacen, Zekk. Yes, even Jaina and Lowie. Master Skywalker, too. Why hadn't she seen it before? Maybe she'd just been too busy believing the lies Czethros told her; she'd lied to herself too much to notice it. Yes, these were her friends. They would help her.

"I need andris. Just one more dose," she pleaded with them. "Then I'll find a way to quit. I promise." The effort of her long speech left her trembling and slumped over in her seat. She didn't see the irony in the fact that she had told herself the same thing last time.

A soft, melodious voice broke through Anja's pain. "There is another way." Ambassador Cilghal stroked a webbed hand against Anja's cheek. "It is more difficult, requires more strength, but it can be done."

Anja shook her head. "Too much pain. I'll die."

"We won't let that happen," Jacen said, more confidence in his words than in his voice.

"How—?" Anja began.

"I am not simply an ambassador," Cilghal answered, "I am a Jedi healer. If you will let me, I can draw the toxins from your blood."

"Will that end the addiction?" Zekk asked.

Cilghal shook her fishy head. "I can take away only the poisons of the body. The poisons in her mind she must learn to remove for herself."

Anja shook her head violently, causing pain to flare in her neck. Droplets of sweat flew from side to side. "Too hard."

"You will not be alone," Tenel Ka said.

"We'll be here to help you," Jacen said, clasping her hand tightly. Tenel Ka covered Jacen's hand with hers.

Zekk folded both hands tightly around Anja's left hand. "We'll be right here with you. All of us."

Anja felt an impossible comfort and relief flowing from her friends' hands to hers. At first, she thought the relief must be in her imagination, that her need had fooled her weakened mind. She withdrew her fingers from Zekk's. Instantly the pain in her left hand returned. She gave a wordless gasp and stretched her arm back toward him. When he took Anja's hand this time, she knew the relief was real. It began in her fingers and tingled in cool waves up her arm.

Anja turned her tortured gaze back to Cilghal. "One more dose. Then I'll accept your help."

Cilghal said nothing. She simply folded her flippered hands and stared at Anja with calm resolve.

Tears of pain now streamed down Anja's face along with the perspiration. The pain was unbearable. She *knew* what she needed to do. Deep down, perhaps she had always known.

"You're right," Anja choked at last. "Putting it off won't help. And I can't do this alone." She shuddered. "All right. What do I have to do?"

Cilghal nodded. She gently pushed Anja's seat back until it reclined. Then she placed one flippered hand on her forehead, one on her stomach. Anja felt Zekk, Tenel Ka, and Jacen press close around her. In all of her life, she had never felt such caring . . . or such *pain*.

After the longest and most excruciating half hour

of her entire life, Anja slipped into blissful uncon-
sciousness.

Anja came back awake, blinking her big eyes, with
a strength and alertness that she could not remember experiencing since before she had begun taking
andris.

Andris! To her surprise, though the very thought
of the spice still enticed her, she found she could
withstand its allure. She pushed herself up in her
seat. Around her, the young Jedi were hard at work
trying to repair the damaged minisub.

"How long—?"

Tenel Ka checked the chronometer. "Three-point-
two hours."

Anja rocked back on her elbows in surprise.
"Then it's over? I'm cured?"

Cilghal turned to fix her with a fishy stare. "Not
cured, my child. *Cleansed.* The toxins are gone, but
your body is still capable of experiencing the
craving for spice."

Anja accepted the news without flinching. Then
she glanced around at Jacen, Zekk, and Tenel Ka,
meeting each pair of eyes in turn. "Thank you for
using your powers to heal me."

Jacen shook his head. "Hey, most of those
powers came from inside *you*. From your wanting
to stay alive and wanting to be healed."

Anja smiled at them all, a warm, genuine smile.
"Maybe. But I don't think I'd have found that
strength inside me if I hadn't had friends."

17

GROPING THROUGH THE spice mines' access tunnels, Jaina, Lowie, and Em Teedee decided that their next step would be to liberate Nien Nunb and his loyal workers. With the help of the prisoners, maybe they could retake Kessel.

Throughout the previous hours, they had heard teams marching up and down the main tunnels, shouting to each other, shining bright glowlamps into dark corners. Judging from the angry tones Jaina heard, the destruction of the transmitter had been a complete success! She could tell that Czethros had stepped up his efforts to find them . . . but the mercenary teams were so loud and clumsy, only a fool would be unable to avoid them.

Jaina and Lowbacca were no fools.

The advantage to the young Jedi, now that Black Sun had all of its resources dedicated to finding the mysterious saboteurs, was that there were too few troops to keep careful watch on the captives. Only one guard remained standing in front of the security field by the prison quarters where Nien Nunb and the Kessel workers were held.

Peeking from the shadows of a low access tunnel, Jaina observed the lone guard near the shimmering stun-field. The guard was gray-skinned, with a long lantern jaw, smooth lipless mouth, and sunken orange eyes. He looked as if he had been dead for some time and had begun to mummify, but Jaina decided this must be what his species looked like. The guard carried only a small blaster at his side. Although either of the two young Jedi could easily have dispatched him with their lightsabers, Jaina preferred to do this without killing. Instead, she thought, this was a perfect time for them to use their Jedi powers.

Quietly she whispered her plan to Lowie, and the two companions concentrated, reaching out with their minds through the Force and probing until they touched the glimmering consciousness of the guard. They sent messages of relaxation to place him into a suggestible state of calm, partially hypnotized, partially asleep.

When they stepped out into the open hall, he spotted them and reacted, nearly making them lose control of his mind. Jaina strode forward quickly. "I wouldn't move, sir—especially not if I had a Kessel scorpion-rat on my shoulder . . . one that's prepared to sting."

The guard glanced down, and his sunken orange

eyes widened in shock and dismay. In his imagination, he saw the horrible crablike creature resting on the shoulder pad of his uniform, its segmented tail and wicked hooked stinger poised and dripping with a deadly greenish venom.

He wailed and thrashed around. "Get it off! Get it off!"

Lowie rushed forward. Instead of drawing his blaster against the oncoming Wookiee, the guard swatted again and again at his neck and upper arm, as if he continued to see the hideous creature scuttling back and forth there.

Lowie grasped the guard by both shoulders and pushed him into the pulsing stun-field that held the prisoners hostage. The guard raised his hands as crackling sparks flew all around, then slumped backward onto the floor, unconscious.

"Easy enough," Jaina said.

"It may require significantly greater skill to break through these Black Sun security codes," Em Teedee said.

"Maybe," Jaina answered, looking over at Lowie. "But then, I've got you two to help."

Nien Nunb and the other spice mine workers, seeing what had happened, clamored and cheered from the other side of the security barricade. They knew they were about to be rescued.

Within moments Lowie and Em Teedee had succeeded in switching off the stun-field. The crackling shimmer in the air faded, and Nien Nunb and his companions rushed out. Smiling and laughing, they clapped each other on the back and offered profuse thanks to Jaina and Lowie.

As Jaina looked at the crowd of former captives now loose in the spice mines, she knew the tide was turning. At first, Czethros had used armed guards and the element of surprise to imprison them. But the tables were turned now, and his advantage was lost.

Czethros had a lot more to worry about than just two young Jedi Knights.

While most of the guards continued to comb through distant and isolated spice tunnels in search of the fugitives, Nien Nunb led the escapees to a main armory and control chamber, protected from outside attack, near the darkest and least used of the excavation shafts. Here his people would be able to pick up supplies, arm themselves, and prepare for the fight to retake Kessel.

Together, they entered the deeply buried control chamber. Once inside, Nien Nunb keyed his administrative codes into the computers. With a blur of furry fingers, he punched in commands. Lowie assisted, growling and offering suggestions. Rapidly, block by block, the Sullustan Chief Administrator denied access to Czethros and his takeover crew.

Cheering, the workers gathered up their weapons and requested permission to return to their quarters to make sure the invaders had not destroyed or commandeered their private possessions. Kessel was a dreary assignment for many of them; they couldn't bear the thought of Black Sun mercenaries pawing through their personal effects. Regretfully, the Chief Administrator shook his head.

Jaina paced the floor of the control center, still anxious, knowing they weren't safe yet. They had a long fight ahead of them to drive the invaders from Kessel. "Can we use this room as our base of operations?" she said. "It's well guarded and we can take care of it."

Nien Nunb nodded.

"Perfect." She explained how she and Lowie had successfully sabotaged the communications array so that the Black Sun plans could not proceed. Things were already falling apart for Czethros, and now that his prisoners were freed, this resistance would be the last straw.

Nien Nunb turned back to his computer console, satisfied with what he had accomplished, and brought up the security holocam images. Lowie rumbled a warning. Figures were moving down the tunnel, sporting weapons and dark uniforms—led by the treacherous Second Administrator Kymn! Directly beside him strode the smiling blond-haired captain who had lied about being impressed with Nien Nunb's part in destroying the Death Star at the Battle of Endor.

The Sullustan made a thin growling sound in his throat and jabbered brief instructions, telling everyone to stay alert. He would take care of this instantly—he had his own score to settle.

"But whatever shall *we* do?" Em Teedee said.

"I think we'll just have to be prepared—for anything," Jaina answered.

Workers brought up their weapons and made ready for a fight as the Chief Administrator scuttled out the door of the control center and down the dark and winding corridors. Nien Nunb felt anger blazing inside him—a new sensation for the timid Sullustan. He vowed to show that blond-haired captain just how a hero really handled himself.

He hustled along, moving with determination . . . trying belatedly to figure out his plan. Kymn's crew of searchers would be surprised to see him free, since they were simply hunting for one or two hidden saboteurs: Jaina and Lowbacca. Or so they thought.

Nien Nunb turned the next corner—and froze stock-still as the treacherous Second Administrator and the blond-haired captain cried out in surprise.

"He's escaped!" Kymn yelled. "Grab him! No— *shoot*!"

"I thought Czethros wanted him kept alive as a hostage," the blond captain said as the guards surged forward.

"Don't trouble yourself," Kymn sneered. "This little rodent has been bossing me around in various jobs for too many years. I'd like the pleasure of seeing *him* squirm for a change."

Black Sun mercenaries charged forward. Reacting with a panic that was only the slightest bit feigned, Nien Nunb squealed and whirled. He pelted back down the low, dim corridor.

Laughing and shouting, believing their quarry had no chance against them, the guards gave chase, led by the bellowing Second Administrator and the captain.

When Nien Nunb rounded the last corner before the control chamber, though, he ducked to one side and pressed himself against the cool rock wall near the door. His loyal fellow prisoners surged out, weapons ready. The two young Jedi Knights stood with pulsating lightsabers.

The opposing guards tumbled into each other, piling up as they scrambled backward in a panic. They had expected no resistance at all. Thinking Kessel secure, Czethros had already reassigned his best mercenaries to other potential battles out in the New Republic. But his own base of operations was the weakest point.

The freed prisoners shouted and aimed their weapons. Blaster fire rang out, cracking walls and spouting tongues of rock dust and smoke. The surprised invaders returned fire, scorching the arm of one of Nien Nunb's defenders—but Second Administrator Kymn quickly realized the ambush had caught them in a very bad situation. Two of his mercenaries fell, writhing in pain. Nien Nunb's fighters kept to their sheltered positions, while Kymn's troops remained completely exposed.

Second Administrator Kymn yelled, "Go left! Move down this way!"

Shots rang out, fired by the turning guards more in confusion and anger than in defense. None of the bolts hit their targets. Broken rock showered from the walls. Nien Nunb's workers fired back, scorching the backplate of one of the retreating Black Sun guards. After only a minor flurry of blaster bolts, the dust settled. No one seemed injured.

The Black Sun forces had fled.

Nien Nunb's defenders charged after the retreating guards, raising their voices. Their howls echoed in the tunnels as Kymn's team rushed away into the deepest spice mines. Nien Nunb shouted at the top of his squeaking voice, and the defenders reluctantly pulled back, letting the mercenaries run onward in the dark tunnels.

Back in the control chamber, the Sullustan Chief Administrator busily entered codes and punched in more commands. Loud metal doors clanged shut deep in the passageways. Lowbacca chuffed with laughter.

Jaina peered down at the screens to see what he had done. "You mean they're all sealed down in those tunnels?"

Nien Nunb's thickly folded lips curved in a smile. Through Em Teedee's translation, he explained that such deep sections of mines could be sealed off at the senior administrator's discretion. Kymn and his guards would remain trapped behind heavy plasteel barricades, where they could cause no trouble. The legitimate security forces on Kessel would eventually get back to them, once they finished mopping up all the other problems here in the spice mines.

The mood was elation. The defenders cheered their first victory. It had been simple and bloodless. Still, Jaina felt uneasy. There was at least one major obstacle left: Czethros himself.

18

OVER THE PAST hour, the temperature had dropped dramatically inside the trapped minisub. Ice walls clasped the *Elfa* like a clenched fist.

The only light that trickled in was a filtered crystalline blue-green from the polar ice pack. Zekk feared that before long the air in the sub would grow thick as well. Deprived of oxygen, filled with carbon dioxide, the atmosphere would offer less and less for its five imprisoned passengers to breathe.

He crawled up to his waist into the *Elfa*'s engine compartment, wriggling his head and arms through the small access hatch. Normally, Calamarian repair crews would either have hoisted the sub into its dock on Crystal Reef or labored underwater to complete repairs. Here, though, Zekk had to make do with what access he could gain from within the cramped cabin.

He had to use a too-small hydrospanner, one of

the few tools available in the meager emergency repair kit. He could see how the gears had ground together, how the electrical connections had been broken and the precise flow conduits knocked out of alignment during the tentacled sea creature's attack. He nudged and tweaked and banged with the hydrospanner, straightening out what he could.

Jacen hovered behind him. "I wish Jaina were here. She's always good at fixing things."

Zekk banged with the hydrospanner again, discouraged, and skinned his knuckles instead. "I'm not such a bad mechanic myself," he said. "And these aren't exactly ideal conditions, you know."

"Not ideal," Anja agreed. "Besides, if Jaina were here, we'd have one more set of lungs using up what's left of our oxygen."

Tenel Ka frowned at the young woman's remark.

"I guess you're right," Zekk said. "I feel better knowing she's safe on Kessel."

Jacen gave Tenel Ka a lopsided grin. "Yeah, my sister's probably just relaxing, bored to tears while we're stuck with all the troubles."

Zekk reattached the connections to the small engines as best he could, using his sore fingers when the tool itself wouldn't work. "Try it now, Cilghal," he called over his shoulder. Then he backed out of the access compartment, his clothes and hands and face grimed with engine lubricants and dust.

The Calamarian ambassador worked at the controls. With a thrumming, puttering growl, the mini-sub's engines fired up. Propellers turned, then ground to a halt against the solid ice that pressed in around them.

"Seems to be working smoothly enough," Jacen said.

"Yes, but we are not able to move anywhere," Tenel Ka pointed out. She listened to the sound of ice scraping against the hull.

"If those icebergs shift, our situation will become even more perilous," Cilghal said. "We'll be crushed."

"Great," Jacen answered. "Up until now I was having a tough time imagining how things could possibly get any worse."

Her face grim, Tenel Ka stood. "We are trapped . . . but it is only ice." She looked around at the four other passengers crowded into the small sub. "I count five lightsabers among us. Certainly that should suffice to cut us free." She raised her eyebrows. "If we are willing to go outside."

Per regulations from the Crystal Reef Amusement and Tourism Council, the minisub was required to carry enough slicksuits for each passenger in an emergency. Their current situation, Jacen thought, was about as much of an emergency as anyone could have imagined.

"You know this is probably suicidal, don't you?" Anja said as she slipped into the flimsy garment that clung to her skin like a symbiotic organism. She pulled the skull-fitting hood over her voluminous hair, so that most of her head was covered. The glistening Calamarian fabric molded itself to bodily contours and provided temperature control. Jacen wondered, though, if even the most efficient heaters would keep them warm enough this deep under the polar ice.

Cilghal stepped forward and took hold of a flap at the neck of Jacen's suit. "This membrane will allow you to breathe," she said, stretching it tight over his mouth and nose. Now only his eyes were exposed. "It will filter oxygen molecules from the water. You can breathe as usual. Just do it slowly and carefully."

"Are you sure our lightsabers will function underwater?" Zekk asked, looking at his newly made—and untested—weapon.

Cilghal nodded, her round Calamarian eyes swiveling as she held up her own lightsaber. The hilt was lumpy, but with a smooth, pearly finish. "It will, if you constructed it properly."

Tenel Ka frowned down at her lightsaber, made from a carved rancor's tooth, and flashed a glance over at Jacen. Zekk knew she must be recalling the day her own defective lightsaber had failed, resulting in the loss of her arm. But she had built a new weapon, taking extra precautions.

Zekk thought of the extraordinary care with which he had built his new lightsaber. Master Skywalker himself had approved. He took a deep breath, nodding confidently. "Then my weapon won't fail."

Jacen, Zekk, Tenel Ka, Anja, and Cilghal finished suiting up, then took turns going through the force-field doorway into the deep, cold ocean. Jacen inhaled deeply. The membrane that covered his face produced a warm flow of breathable air.

Still, he hesitated at the portal. Anja, standing next to him, gave him an inquiring look. Finally, Jacen stepped through the shimmering hatch and out into a world of liquid ice.

Pulsing lightsaber blades blazed through the water like colorful torches, attracting tiny darting fish that somehow lived and flourished in the inhospitable arctic environment. Stalactites of clear blue ice lurked around them like massive fangs. Broken icebergs trapped the insignificant minisub. The lightsabers shimmered in the murky water, cutting an underwater channel through the frozen mountains.

With her one arm—the other sleeve snubbed tightly and knotted so it would be waterproof— Tenel Ka wielded her turquoise blade. She slashed, severing a slab of ice. Steam and bubbles erupted as the chunk slowly drifted away, freeing one of the fins of the minisub.

Jacen hacked and chopped at the prison of ice. His lungs heaved, drawing tendrils of air through the membrane. All around him the water felt like a smothering blanket of carbonite. The slicksuit fought off most of the deadly chill, but the cold eventually seeped through. Jacen found his arms and legs growing sluggish. His mind felt lethargic and stupid, as if he were thinking in slow motion.

Cilghal, better adapted for underwater work even in the arctic seas, swam ahead, using her throbbing lightsaber to hack her way forward. Bubbles churned upward until they were trapped by the ice ceiling. Cilghal cleared a narrow channel, then moved along the fresh passageway, rolling with her lightsaber.

Zekk swam directly behind her, widening the channel with his energy blade.

Jacen, Tenel Ka, and Anja worked closer to the *Elfa*. When the last of the frozen jaws were sheared away, the small craft settled slightly and drifted loose. Jacen felt the cold growing more and more intense all around his body. His arms and legs seemed heavy. Too heavy.

Tenel Ka watched him with a look of concern. They were both good swimmers. Together they had spent many days swimming in the river on Yavin 4. But this was *cold*, infinitely colder. . . .

Jacen forced his hand to give a thumbs-up sign, and Tenel Ka nodded. Together they swam back toward the minisub's force-field hatch. Jacen waved for Anja, who floated in place close to the *Elfa* holding her acid-yellow lightsaber. She signaled that she would be behind them in a moment. Jacen and Tenel Ka rapidly stroked toward the hatch, toward warmth.

Up ahead, Cilghal and Zekk had nearly finished with their labors as well.

Anja had worked as hard as she could manage. She had no strength in the Force, and her only special abilities with a lightsaber had come from having her body pumped up with andris spice. She was free of that addiction now, however. She would never use the spice again . . . but that also meant she would never feel the same rush again, the energy she had once considered a part of her strength.

The lightsaber in her hand was a fraud, nothing more than an antique she had purchased from a peddler who specialized in Jedi artifacts. Anja knew how hard Zekk had worked to build his own sleek and simple weapon—and its hilt looked nothing like the heavy, ornate design of her energy blade.

However, Zekk's lightsaber was *real*. He had earned his, and he knew how to use it. The Force guided him. Anja's didn't belong to her, no matter what she had paid for it. It was a Jedi weapon, and she was not—nor would she ever be—a Jedi. Perhaps the lightsaber was itself a symbol of her addiction—her willingness to rely on something that was not a part of her.

Caught up in her restless thoughts, she swam around the fin of the minisub and saw something trapped between two struts in the support casing that held the rudder in place: a single remaining vial of andris spice, glittering and preserved in the frigid water. It must have caught there when they broke open the containers hidden under the ice caps, or when the sea monster had attacked them and consumed the rest of the stash.

As if drawn by a magnet, Anja swam forward and plucked out the vial. It was pure andris.

Anja hesitated. She could take it . . . treat herself to one last dose.

She felt the yearning return inside her, a longing for that familiar surge of energy that made her feel so intensely alive. She knew it was more mental than physical. If she succumbed now, if she kept this dose for herself . . . it would be like voluntarily placing her hands into a set of stun-cuffs. She might as well lock herself up and become a prisoner of her own addiction once more.

But Anja didn't want that. She didn't want it ever again.

She let the vial drift out of her hand. The small object floated there in front of her, taunting her, daring her to change her mind.

Anja locked her acid-yellow lightsaber ON and, with an effort, swept down, slicing through the offensive vial. It disintegrated in a puff of seared materials.

Then, as she stared down at the Jedi relic in her grasp, Anja knew she could never use it again. Deep inside, she felt a calm finality at this knowledge.

Anja's cold fingers released their grip on the hilt and let the lightsaber drift away. Then, with a feeling of satisfaction, Anja swam back to the warmth and companionship that waited for her aboard the minisub.

19

CZETHROS WAS ON the run. He could see no way out of his situation.

If he managed to escape Kessel and elude the young Jedi Knights and Nien Nunb's security team, he might be even worse off . . . because then he would have to explain this failure to his brutal superiors in Black Sun. Czethros was certain those people could think of much more imaginative punishments than any New Republic justice organization could. Even his old nemesis, Han Solo, would probably be more kind.

With the signal generator destroyed, Czethros had no way to rally his scattered forces around the galaxy. The few operatives he had planted in appropriate positions of power controlled key systems—but unless everything happened simultaneously at Czethros's command, it would all come to naught. The few isolated emergencies would easily be dealt with by the New Republic.

His chance had now been lost. Even his grasp on the spice mines of Kessel had slipped. Instead of orchestrating the sudden overthrow of industries and minor governments across what remained of the Empire, Czethros found himself running for his life. Hiding in the dark mines. Humiliated.

The tide had turned. Nien Nunb and his security troops controlled the catacombs. Second Administrator Kymn and the other infiltrators Czethros had planted here had either been captured or otherwise neutralized.

Perhaps if he could get to a docking bay, he could steal a ship and get away. Perhaps Czethros could make a new life for himself, hiding somewhere in the Outer Rim. He didn't seem to have much of a chance, but it was better than waiting here. And it was better than letting himself get caught by Black Sun.

As silently as possible, he crawled up ladders, rung by rung. He wasn't used to such physical exertion. During all the many years he had been running the show on Ord Mantell, he hadn't had to fend for himself much. He'd always had droids or henchmen.

But now Czethros was alone. He knew he could trust no one.

Furtively, he consulted one of the electronic wall maps of the spice mines. The projection grids were frequently out of date, since new shafts were always being drilled and new excavations dug. But the main docking bays were permanent structures, and so most of the directions remained valid.

Czethros followed narrow ventilation shafts. He felt uneasy, as if he were a poisonous insect creeping into a peaceful home, but he had to get to an empty ship and escape somehow.

When he emerged into the main cargo bay, he poked his head out of the shadows to make certain he could move without being seen. There among the stranded empty spaceships he spotted a little man moving about, tinkering with the engines on his craft. Czethros recognized him as the hapless and not terribly bright smuggler, Lilmit.

The small man used his webbed fingers to fiddle with the external flow controls, and the sublight engines sent out a bright blast. Then the repulsors made a rewarding and satisfying hum. Lilmit jumped up and down with glee.

Czethros's heart swelled with hope. *This* was what he needed to see. He marched forward, squaring his shoulders to look as intimidating as possible. Lilmit was his employee, someone he could easily manipulate.

Czethros crossed the docking bay floor. Lilmit didn't even notice him until the Black Sun lieutenant was nearly at his side. "Keep those engines running, Lilmit," he said. "You and I are going to get out of here—right now."

The small smuggler squawked. "Czethros! I was just leaving! What happened to your takeover?"

"There's been a change. Nien Nunb has regained control—and you are going to help me escape."

"But then they'll chase after my ship. I have only minimal weapons and—"

"I'm offering you a great honor, Lilmit. Don't let me down."

Just then, shouts erupted from the far side of the docking bay. Han Solo's brat Jaina, the Wookiee Lowbacca, the meddling Chief Administrator Nien Nunb, and some troops from the Kessel guard forces surged into the docking bay.

"There now. You see?" Em Teedee chirped. "I tracked his voice via the station audio system! Didn't I tell you he would be here?"

"Czethros, halt!" one of the guard captains shouted.

Nien Nunb chattered something loud and harsh in Sullustan. Jaina and Lowie powered up their lightsabers.

Lilmit squealed in terror and scrambled up the boarding ramp of his ship faster than Czethros had ever seen a panicked rodent move. The Black Sun lieutenant turned, knowing that Lilmit now had no choice but to get them out of there.

But as he moved toward the hatch, hydraulics roared and the heavy door slammed shut in his face. With a hissing sound, the pressure seal engaged. Lights winked on, indicating that access was no longer possible.

With a roar of rage, Czethros pounded on the outer door. "Lilmit, let me in!" He heard only a distant squeak of terror. The Kessel guards rushed forward, and Czethros knew he could not stand and argue with the treacherous little coward.

Spotting an open turbolift to one side of the docking bay, he ran at full speed. He was closer to it than his pursuers.

Some of the guards fired blaster bolts, only a few of them set on "stun." He dodged. Sparking bolts ricocheted off the insulated walls. Czethros dove headfirst into the turbolift and activated it.

The guards ran toward him, howling with frustration at losing him again. The door hissed shut. Czethros felt the floor drop out from under him as he plunged down, down into the deepest mines.

"Where does that turbolift go?" Jaina shouted, her face flushed from the exertion of the chase.

The Sullustan administrator jabbered an answer, and Em Teedee politely translated. "Master Nien Nunb says that turbolift is a direct link to the new andris spice processing facility. He calls it an 'express tube.' It would appear that Czethros is heading directly down to the new assembly lines and carbonite chambers."

"How do we catch up with him?" Jaina cried.

The Sullustan chittered, and Em Teedee said, "Because of the recent addition of the carbonite-freezing facilities for the andris spice, Master Nien Nunb had a second, freight-only turbolift installed to handle the increased load."

Lowie roared and pointed to an adjacent turbolift. The mousy administrator nodded.

"Well, what are we waiting for?" Jaina was already rushing toward the open doors.

Crowded with Nien Nunb, Lowbacca, Jaina, Em Teedee, and several guards, the turbolift plummeted. Since this lift was designed primarily for hauling cargo at high speed, the passengers were forced to hang on for dear life. Fortunately, the group was so tightly packed that there was little room for jostling about.

As soon as the doors whisked open again, a blaster bolt streaked into the turbolift. Jaina and Lowie ducked. A guard cried out as a scorching bolt singed the shoulder of his uniform.

Jaina and Lowie dove out and rolled as they hit the floor. Keeping low, they crept around the equipment in the assembly line. They could see the polished black legs of the blind beetles that worked there. The sharp insectoid limbs were suddenly thrown into a frenzy as the unexpected violence disrupted their daily work.

Czethros blasted one of the beetles. Its shell split open, and it fell dead beside one of the open vats of raw carbonite, clacking its jaws. Steaming green ooze poured from the smoking wound. Another wild bolt shattered vials of andris on the conveyor belt line, and the machinery groaned to a halt. Sparks and smoke filled the air. The Kessel guards took up defensive positions, laying siege to the lone fugitive.

"Czethros, you can't get away now. Give yourself up," Jaina said. Lowie roared, adding his encouragement.

Czethros did not surrender. Instead, more blaster fire rang out from where he had hidden himself between the bubbling vats of carbonite and their monitoring systems.

"Dear me! It would appear that he doesn't wish to be taken alive," Em Teedee said.

"I'd rather *not* kill him," Jaina said. "I'm hoping the New Republic'll find him a nice comfortable prison cell off on an asteroid somewhere. But first we have to capture him." She raised her voice. "We know all about your plan, Czethros! You can't send your signal. Black Sun has failed. It's over."

"Maybe," Czethros bellowed back. "But we've still got a thousand traitors in a thousand important positions throughout the New Republic. You'll never figure out who they are. Someone else will pick up the plan."

Jaina wondered if he wanted to bargain with them, but she didn't have that kind of authority, nor did anyone here. They would just have to capture him and let the New Republic deal with his crimes. "That's possible," she said, "but right now the entire plan is useless without your coordination. We'll ferret your people out sooner or later."

One of the guards shouted, "Why don't you surrender, Czethros? It's the only way you'll come out alive."

"Black Sun will kill me no matter what prison you choose. I don't have a chance anyway."

"But we could try to protect you," the guard argued. Lowbacca roared, urging Czethros to come out.

"All right then. I'll surrender." Czethros's answer came too easily; Jaina sensed a subtle devious intent in his voice. "I'm holding out my weapon. I'm coming out. *Don't shoot*."

Czethros slowly eased from his sheltered position between equipment, moving around boxlike storage alcoves, cabinets, and engine housings. He held his blaster in front of him, carefully pointing it away from all the others. They watched uneasily as he crept forward, edging along the side of the carbonite vat where the dead beetle he had gunned down still sprawled.

His face looked cloudy, uncertain, just the way a prisoner's should. The moment the majority of the guards had lowered their weapons by the merest fraction, Czethros rolled, swung up his blaster rifle, and stepped sideways, screaming, "You won't take me alive!"

But as he let fly a full-power blast from the rifle, his foot came down in a pool of slick, oozing green blood from the beetle he had killed. He slipped and stumbled over the carcass. With a loud cry, his blaster rifle firing harmlessly toward the ceiling, Czethros lurched backward—and fell into the open vat. The carbonite enveloped him in its fog of absolute, penetrating cold.

Tendrils of white vapor whirled up as the carbonite made quick work of the Black Sun lieutenant.

In an instant, Czethros was frozen solid . . . perfectly preserved by the frothing liquid.

Grumbling, Lowie crept forward to stand carefully at the edge of the vat. Guards stood in shock. Nien Nunb chattered under his breath, not sure what to do.

Lowie looked down into the swirling, metallic-gray currents and mumbled something. He felt the unrelenting cold waft up to freeze the fur on his face.

Jaina agreed. "You're right, Lowie. This *is* one way to capture him."

20

THE MINISUB THAT sailed back into the artificial harbor at Crystal Reef was as battered as any starship Zekk had ever seen survive a space battle. Before the companions could even emerge from the *Elfa*, the treelike harbormaster was there on the dock beside it, making horrified exclamations. To Zekk's absolute amazement, however, the Yarin's expressions of concern were for the passengers, not his damaged ship.

Still fussing and exclaiming, the Yarin ushered them past the queue of waiting customers and into his office. The look of dismay on the treelike alien's face was truly comical, and he waved and rustled his branched arms. Without asking for an explanation, the harbormaster ordered hot drinks and soft warm robes for each of the returned passengers.

"I can't tell you how sorry I am that your undersea experience here at Crystal Reef was not everything that you had hoped." The Yarin eyed their injuries with some trepidation: Zekk's cut and blistered fingers from working in the engine compartment with insufficient tools, the lump on his forehead, the bruise on Tenel Ka's cheek from a chuck of floating ice . . .

"I assure you we'll attend to your medical needs immediately, but if there's anything else I can do to make it up—"

"Please," Ambassador Cilghal broke in gently, "it is we who should apologize. In our enthusiasm to explore the polar ice cap, we neglected to take into account the . . . appetites of some of the ocean's larger denizens."

With a look of wonder, the Yarin leaned toward her. "Tell me. What happened?"

Cilghal, with the help of Zekk, Jacen, Tenel Ka, and Anja, told the story of their encounter with the mighty sea creature, strategically leaving out all information about the andris spice. After all, the Jedi did not know who at Crystal Reef might be working for Black Sun. The Yarin listened with rapt attention, asking a series of probing questions and delighting in their answers.

"Then it's true," he said at last. "You actually saw a Great Arctic Skra'akan and survived to tell of it." His voice held a tone of awe. "Did you perhaps capture the event with a holocam?"

"Not intentionally," Tenel Ka replied.

"We were all kind of occupied at the time," Jacen added.

"I guess we didn't realize what a big event it was," Anja admitted.

Zekk thought for a moment. "I don't suppose the *Elfa*'s equipped with one of those microholocams that makes a complete record of a trip in case some sort of disaster happens?"

The Yarin's face lit with excitement. "Yes, of course! I use it as a supplementary log. I cannot wait to review the recordings! It is good luck, you know, to see a Great Arctic Skra'akan."

Anja gave him a wry smile. "Well, we're lucky to be alive. Does that count?"

Cilghal looked at her battered companions. Jacen wondered if they would have to edit the images of destroying the spice stockpile, or if the Ambassador would classify the tapes.

"Your . . . Skra'akan, was it? . . . got pretty violent there for a while," Jacen said.

A look of apprehension dawned in the bulky harbormaster's eyes. "You didn't . . ."

"Kill it?" Zekk said. "No. In fact the last time we saw the creature, I have no doubt he was still happily imagining us as his next meal."

The Yarin gave a satisfied sigh. "Then all is well."

Cilghal took a long drink from her mug and said, "There's still the matter of payment for the damage to your vessel."

The harbormaster waved a branchlike arm. "Think nothing of it. If you truly brought back images of a Great Arctic Skra'akan, I believe that the *Elfa* and those holos may become a permanent tourist exhibit here at Crystal Reef.

"Besides"—he dropped his voice to a tone of confidentiality—"the administration of Crystal Reef has promised me that if Jedi Master Skywalker, the Chief of State and her husband, or the rulers of the Hapes cluster make an official visit to Crystal Reef thanks to your efforts here, I will be rewarded with *two* new minisubmersibles of my choice."

Jacen grinned at him. "Great! We'll just have to see what we can do to arrange that."

After Crystal Reef's medical droids had treated their injuries, the companions thanked the harbormaster again for his assistance. Promising to meet Jacen and Tenel Ka back on Kessel, Zekk and Anja said their thanks and good-byes to Cilghal and went to retrieve the *Lightning Rod* from the docking bay where Anja had left it. Zekk was glad to be back behind the controls of his own ship again.

Cilghal took Tenel Ka and Jacen in the wave-skimmer and headed back to her floating city, where the *Rock Dragon* waited for them.

"Jacen, my friend. I have been meaning to ask you something," Tenel Ka said in a serious tone as the waveskimmer carried them across the ocean. "Would you consent to be my . . . copilot?"

Jacen's lopsided grin was instant and enthusiastic. "I thought you'd never ask."

The journey back to Kessel passed much too quickly for both of them. Their conversation was constant and interesting, and Tenel Ka even encouraged Jacen to tell a few jokes. He teased her throughout the trip, and when he called her "Captain," a smile of amusement curved the corners of her mouth.

"Remind me to give you something when we get back to Yavin 4," Jacen said as he and Tenel Ka brought the *Rock Dragon* down through Kessel's thin atmosphere toward the docking bay that ground control had just approved for them.

She arched an eyebrow at him. "What shall I tell you to give me?"

Jacen felt his face grow warm. "Just something I made for you. I've kind of been waiting for the right time."

The next few minutes were occupied with landing procedures. Jacen, who hadn't often seen Tenel Ka pilot a ship, was surprised and pleased at how well she handled the *Rock Dragon*. The landing was smooth, clean, and uneventful.

"Back to boring old Kessel," Jacen said. "I could use a bit of a rest."

The *Lightning Rod* was berthed next to the *Rock Dragon*. Between the two ships, Jacen was amazed to see Jaina, Lowie, Zekk, *and Anja* exchanging warm hugs of greeting. Nien Nunb was there too, and Em Teedee hovered about, happily providing translations for anyone who needed them.

As Jacen and Tenel Ka disembarked in the industrial-looking docking bay, Zekk looked up at

Jacen and shrugged. "I've already apologized to Jaina for not coming to her rescue."

"Why?" Jacen said. "Because she was so *bored*?"

Lowie roared an objection. Jaina punched her brother on the arm. "*Bored?* While you all were off on your little pleasure cruise," she said, a teasing look in her brandy-brown eyes, "*we* were busy trying to save half the major businesses in the galaxy from a hostile takeover by Black Sun."

Lowie gave a roar for emphasis. "Indeed," Em Teedee said. "You have absolutely no idea how much we have to tell you."

21

WITH THE CRISIS finally over, the return trip from Kessel to the Jedi academy was uneventful. The companions—Zekk, Jaina, and Anja in the *Lighting Rod*, and Tenel Ka, Jacen, Lowie, and Em Teedee aboard the *Rock Dragon*—spent the time exchanging stories of their adventures.

When they all arrived at the landing field on Yavin 4, with its lush jungle surrounding the spectacular ancient pyramids, Master Skywalker himself was there to welcome them back.

Wearing a mock-stern expression on his face, the Jedi Master looked around at the young Jedi Knights and Anja and Em Teedee. "I just received an enlightening message from a former student of mine on Mon Calamari, Ambassador Cilghal. I'm not sure I understand *why* the administration at Crystal Reef wants me and Han and Leia to take an all-expense-paid vacation there."

Luke pursed his lips and gave a slow bemused shake of his head. "And I got a glowing message a few minutes ago from Nien Nunb on Kessel. He thanked me repeatedly for allowing you to stay long enough to help him fix his transmitter . . . ?"

He shook his head again, as if he could hardly believe what he had heard. "I *thought* I sent all of you out to find a friend who was in trouble—not to save the entire New Republic from a hostile financial takeover." The stern set of his lips softened into a proud smile. "I wonder if I'll ever stop being surprised by the things my students manage to accomplish when they work together."

The companions looked at each other, somewhat embarrassed.

"Anyway, now I have a surprise for *you*. The New Republic has decided to hold a celebration here in a few days—and it's about time, after all the work you've done. I think you're all going to receive some long-overdue appreciation, after defeating the Shadow Academy and thwarting the Diversity Alliance, and now Black Sun. Our first guests should be here by evening meal. But before they start arriving, I'd like the chance to speak with each of you alone. We have some important issues to discuss about your future. All of you."

"Luke—Master Skywalker?" Anja spoke hesitantly. "If you wouldn't mind, sir, I'd like to be first."

The Jedi Master looked into her large eyes for a

long moment and then nodded. "I see you've come a long way."

By twilight the entire Jedi academy was in a state of controlled pandemonium. Excitement and anticipation hung in the air like rich perfumes. Cooks and Jedi trainees and even New Republic security guards bustled back and forth in the kitchens, helping to serve the guests who were already beginning to fill the Great Temple.

With a minimum of the usual fanfare that accompanied the travels of the Chief of State, the *Millennium Falcon* showed up in time for evening meal, carrying Jacen and Jaina's parents, their younger brother Anakin, Chewbacca, and the golden protocol droid See-Threepio. Jacen made a point of sitting next to his father as the Solo family ate their first meal together in months. While Jaina was busy explaining how Czethros had schemed to trigger a revolution of sorts via transmitter, Jacen spoke quietly with Han.

"I know I've been kind of a jerk, halfway believing you murdered Anja's father because of how she told the story, and I'm sorry. I guess she was just so hurt and angry all the time, I figured there had to be a reason."

Han raised his eyebrows. "And I was that reason?"

Jacen shrugged. "Well, Anja believed you were."

"And you believed Anja." Han's face became more stern.

"Not anymore," Jacen said. "I've known you all my life, and you've never lied to me. Well, maybe *exaggerated* sometimes—but only for dramatic effect. Anyhow, I should have known you were telling the truth."

"A pretty girl with a pair of sad eyes can make it hard to see the truth sometimes," Han observed.

"Yeah," Jacen admitted, squirming a bit. "But hey, that's no excuse. I'm sorry I doubted you."

Han put an arm around Jacen's shoulder and gave him a brief hug. "Thanks, kid. You've got no idea how good it feels to hear you say that. Really makes me feel like we're a family again."

Jacen felt as if a weight had been lifted from his mind. He grinned around like an idiot at his father and mother, then at Jaina and Anakin. Anakin's ice-blue eyes were rolled to one side in that odd expression he wore when solving a puzzle. Around them, the buzz of conversation in the eating hall rose and fell in random patterns.

"Okay, I think I've got it," Anakin said. "Nothing simpler."

Jaina smiled and ruffled her younger brother's dark hair affectionately. "All right, what does the master puzzle-solver of the galaxy think the solution is?"

"Solution to what?" Jacen wanted to know, reaching over to take a hot bread-puff. Two serving droids hustled in with trays of steaming foods, recipes sure to please the palates of any number of species. He thought briefly of the wild food fight they'd had just after they'd first met Lowbacca—so much had changed in all that time.

Leia spread her hands on the polished table. "We still need to find out who the Black Sun infiltrators and operatives were. I'm hoping to thaw Czethros out from that block of carbonite he's in so that I can question him."

"I'd like to be there when you do that," Han Solo said. Half of his mouth quirked in a wry smile. "I have some experience with carbon-freezing. And besides, Czethros was an old . . . acquaintance of mine."

Leia's dark eyes lit with amusement, and a dimple appeared in her cheek. "Yes, you *might* be of some help. I seem to remember it wasn't easy to get you unfrozen from carbonite and away from Jabba the Hutt. But even if we work together to question Czethros, we don't know if he'll cooperate and give us any names."

"Wait. I have another idea," Anakin said.

"All right, kid, shoot," Han said encouragingly.

Anakin brushed his straight dark bangs away from his piercing blue eyes. "You haven't made any general announcement yet about capturing Czethros, have you?"

Leia shook her head. "I've asked Nien Nunb to keep it quiet. We don't want Black Sun putting out a bounty on Czethros before we have a chance to interrogate him."

"Good." Anakin looked at his sister. "Did Czethros

program in any specific destinations for his message beacons?"

Jaina sighed. "Afraid not. He had the message programmed in, but it's in some sort of unbreakable code. All we managed to learn for sure was the frequency he planned to use."

Anakin clapped his hands. "That should be enough." He directed his gaze back toward his parents. "This could be tricky. Here's what I suggest. Pick a planet and alert the people there that something important is about to happen and to watch for it."

"Go on," Jacen urged, interested in his brother's line of thinking.

"Then we send a message via direct beam *only to that planet*," Anakin said. "Use the message Czethros programmed, and sent it on the frequency he was planning to use." He shrugged. "Then sit back and wait to see what happens."

Han and Leia exchanged hopeful glances.

"Just might work," Han said. "We can fight the little takeovers one at a time, instead of all at once. Black Sun doesn't stand a chance that way."

"I knew I had *one* brother who was a genius," Jaina said with a teasing look at Jacen.

It was Anakin who blushed, though. He shrugged. "The biggest problem with my plan is that you'd probably have to do this dozens of times," he said.

Leia leaned over to give her younger son a kiss on the cheek, then stood briskly. "I guess I'd better get our people started on this right away, in that case. Before word leaks out." She smiled down at her husband. "I'll be in the comm center if you need me." Then she swept out of the room.

That evening, while Leia made strategic arrangements, more visitors poured into the Jedi academy—friends, family, dignitaries, and the occasional HoloNet news reporter. During this time, Anja found a moment to draw Han Solo aside and speak with him.

Han looked decidedly uncomfortable as they sat opposite each other on wooden benches in a small alcove. A narrow window slit in the stone wall let in moonlight that splashed on the floor like a dividing line painted between them.

Anja took a deep breath, knowing that there was much she had to say. She hardly knew where to begin. "I—I never thanked you," she stammered at last.

Obviously surprised, Han Solo sat up straighter. This wasn't what he had expected at all. "For what?" he asked with a hint of suspicion.

"For taking me in. For going to my planet and helping to stop the civil war there. For keeping Lilmit from supplying more weapons to my people. For putting in a good word with Master Skywalker for me, even though I obviously despised you. . . ."

Anja's voice caught in her throat, and she swallowed back a sob of emotion. She remembered how Jacen often tried to lighten the mood when things got tense. "And thanks for not throwing me out the

Millennium Falcon's airlock when you had the chance."

Han Solo seemed to relax a bit. "Hey, no one's perfect. I'm glad I was able to help."

"Your children helped me too."

"They're great kids, Jacen and Jaina," Han said with no small amount of fatherly pride.

"Did you know I tried to turn them against you?"

"It worked a little," Han admitted. "At least with Jacen. But the truth is stronger than hatred."

"I got close to your kids because I wanted to hurt you, because I believed you murdered my father and ruined my life. But once I got to know Jacen and Jaina, I started to understand that if anyone had ruined my life, it was me. I chose the wrong person to trust. I was always looking for someone to blame. I believed Czethros and his lies about you, because I wanted my problems to be somebody else's fault."

"And now?" Han asked.

"I don't want to hurt you anymore," Anja said. "My father was responsible for his own life—and probably for his own death—just like I'm responsible for my life and the way I've decided to live it so far. I judged you before I ever got to know you. Can you . . . forgive me?"

Han nodded. "I had my scoundrel days, too, you know. Did plenty of things I'm not proud of. Even though I didn't kill your father, I have a lot of other things I could feel guilty about. But that's long in my past now—put it all behind me and made a new life. It's possible, you know."

"Yes, I know. Even so, if my friends hadn't trusted me, I wouldn't have believed in myself." Anja felt a sense of relief. But where did she go from here? "I'll have to find a job, I guess. A legal one, that is. I know I'm not cut out to be a Jedi Knight," Anja admitted. "I never used to believe in all that Force mumbo jumbo, but I see now that it's real. It's just not me. I can't stay here at the Jedi academy. Know anyone who needs a good pilot?"

Han put a hand to his chin and thought for a moment. "I just might have a few ideas, at that."

furred brother honored in the ceremony. Raynar's mother, Aryn Dro Thul, and his uncle Tyko—who were assisting the Chief of State in her investigation into Black Sun activities—were also very much in evidence, dressed in formal Alderaan colors as well as the insignias of the Bornaryn trading fleet.

Han and Leia spent as much time with their children as possible between planning sessions for the grand awards ceremony or conducting the Black Sun investigation. Anakin's best friend and fellow student Tahiri had the full attention of the Jedi historian Tionne whenever the silver-haired instructor was not teaching classes. When they were off-duty, even See-Threepio, Artoo-Detoo, and Em Teedee enjoyed long droid conversations together, discussing the merits of various lubricants or the superiority of one type of motivator over another.

Master Skywalker himself welcomed many of his former students who had returned for the festivities. Looking unruffled and serene, he split his time, sometimes visiting with Leia and her family, sometimes catching up on news with former students, sometimes greeting visiting dignitaries, and sometimes encouraging his students and trainees.

On the day of the actual ceremony, in the midst of all the furor, the companions managed to steal away to the platform on the top of the Great Temple and find some quiet time together. Anakin and Tahiri sat at one side of the platform, dangling their bare feet over the edge, while the fluffy creature

Ikrit, their frequent companion, basked in the sun beside them.

At one corner of the platform, Raynar and the cinnamon-maned centaur girl, Lusa, sparred with stunsticks. Lowie, Em Teedee, Jaina, Zekk, and Anja arranged themselves along another side of the platform to watch the busy landing field. Having just finished taking care of his menagerie of animals, Jacen now joined his friends, his fluffy blue pet gort riding on his shoulder. Tenel Ka, just finished with her morning's calisthenics, dashed up one of the staircases at the four corners of the Great Temple to meet them.

When they were all together, Anja said, "I guess this is about as good a time as any to say good-bye. I'll be leaving after the ceremony."

"Why?" Jacen asked, sounding the slightest bit disappointed.

"Because I don't belong here," Anja said. "I've got to do something with my life, but being trained in the Force just isn't it."

"So, where are you going?" Zekk asked.

Anja shrugged. "I'm not sure, but I can't stay at the Jedi academy. I'm not a Jedi. But you all are—you belong together."

"We will not always be together, however," Tenel Ka said. Lowie woofed his agreement.

"Right," Jaina added. "We all just had that long talk with Uncle Luke. You know, the one that goes, 'Now that you're more or less a full Jedi, you have to think about what you want to do in life.'"

Anja gave a wry smile as she threw her silky dark hair behind her shoulder. "That's not exactly the talk I had with him, but it's close enough."

"Well, hello. . . ." A voice from behind startled them all. "Han told me I might be able to find you here."

"Lando!" Jaina jumped up and greeted their visitor with a hug. Lando Calrissian's smile was as brilliant as his flowing cape in the morning sun. "I'd like to thank you all personally for what you did to stop Czethros. Cloud City is perfectly normal again." He gave a slight bow, swirling his colorful cape. "Just like me, there are a lot of lucky business owners in the galaxy whose companies are intact because of what you did. They just don't know it. But *I* do, so I wanted to thank you."

They all assured Lando that he was very welcome.

"Now, since that piece of business is taken care of," Lando went on smoothly, "there's another reason I came up here this morning." His flashing eyes fixed on Anja Gallandro. "My buddy Han tells me you might be in the market for a brand-new job. And *I* just happen to be in the market for a good pilot."

Anja jumped to her feet. Her face looked hopeful, and at the same time slightly suspicious. "I do need a job, but . . ." Her voice trailed off.

"But . . . ?" Lando prompted.

"I was pretty rude to you the last few times we met. I can't believe you'd want to hire me."

Lando flashed his white teeth. "I try not to hold a grudge. Besides, I know what it's like trying to find honest work when you know all you need is a chance." He held out a hand to Anja. "Would you mind being . . . respectable for a while? It's all I've got to offer."

"I'll take it," she said, shaking his hand.

Instead of letting her hand go, Lando smoothly tucked it under his arm and began walking with her toward the stone steps, spilling details of the position. "Now, you understand it doesn't pay much at first, but there's plenty of room to advance in my businesses."

Anja's attention focused completely on Lando. "Fair enough, Calrissian. I can handle that. What about benefits? Do you use incentives? Profit sharing?"

Lando threw back his head and laughed. "Young lady, I can see that we speak the same language."

As they approached the entrance to go down into the Great Temple, Anja looked back at her friends and waved. "I'll see you at the ceremony," she said, then returned her attention to Lando.

As the two disappeared, arm in arm, Jacen heard Anja say, "If you're really interested in giving people a chance to reform, I know this guy named Lilmit. I think he could really use a job, too. . . ."

Jacen grinned. Anja really had come a long way.

"Jacen, my friend?" It was Tenel Ka. "Would now be an appropriate time to ask about the item you intended to give me?"

"Sure. I brought it with me," Jacen said, reaching into the pocket of his rumpled brown jumpsuit. He held the object out to her. Irregular shards of translucent pearly pink dangled from a knotted cord of fine leather. "It's a necklace," he explained unnecessarily. "I made it from the shards of Nicta's gort egg. Many cultures consider it to be very precious—the egg, I mean." The gort sat angelically on his shoulder.

Perhaps it was a trick of the light, but Jacen could have sworn that some sort of liquid shimmered in Tenel Ka's gray eyes when she said, "It is beautiful, Jacen, my friend. Would you please assist me in putting it on?"

Jacen reached both arms beneath her red-gold warrior braids to tie the thong at the back of her neck.

Before he could finish, Tenel Ka pulled him into a strong embrace and said, "I will treasure your gift more than all the rainbow gems of Gallinore."

Zekk put an arm around Jaina. "I don't have a necklace for you, but you can be my copilot—or my pilot—anytime you want."

Resting her head on his shoulder, Jaina chuckled. "Don't think I won't take you up on that. Besides, necklaces aren't exactly my style."

Lowie looked thoughtfully, longingly up at the sky. He rumbled a mellow comment. "Indeed?" Em Teedee replied. "Well, I'm afraid I, for one, shall never understand these humans."

• • •

The grand audience chamber of the Great Temple was filled to overflowing. Thousands of friends, family, dignitaries, students, and other spectators crowded the stone benches. Leia Organa Solo and her husband Han stood with Master Luke Skywalker on the dais at the front of the room, flanked by Chewbacca, Artoo-Detoo, and See-Threepio.

It was the same dais on which they had stood more than two decades ago after the destruction of the first Death Star, to receive special medals from the struggling Rebellion. But this time the former heroes of Yavin were here to honor their children, their nieces and nephews, their students and friends—the new heroes of a new generation.

Stirring music soared through the air and reverberated from the ancient walls. To cheers and applause, Jacen, Jaina, Tenel Ka, Lowie, Zekk, Em Teedee, Anakin, and Anja advanced up the main aisle and climbed the stairs to the platform. As they reached the dais, Master Skywalker welcomed each one with a medal. Next, Leia, Han, and Chewie offered thanks and congratulations on behalf of the New Republic.

The young Jedi Knights, along with Anja and Em Teedee, turned to face the audience. Raynar and Lusa also joined them, recognized for their assistance during the struggle against the misguided Diversity Alliance. Row upon row of friends and loved ones looked up at them with pride.

At a signal from Master Skywalker, the fully

trained Jedi Knights in the first row of the audience drew their lightsabers and switched them on. Then Luke's former students held their glowing energy blades high in blazing tribute to the new heroes before them.

When the crowd had spent a full two minutes roaring in approval, the Jedi historian Tionne quietly moved to the front of the dais at one side. Raising the stringed instrument she carried, the silvery-haired Jedi began to play.

Slowly, a hush fell over the audience, and Tionne lifted her voice in song. Her ballad told of the rise and fall of the Shadow Academy, the defeat of the insidious Diversity Alliance, and how the threat of Czethros and Black Sun had been overcome. The melody carried a message of new hope as Tionne sang of bravery in the face of danger, betrayal and redemption, trust in the Force, and sacrifice.

New legends of the new Jedi.

Turn the page for a preview of the latest book
in the explosive new series from

LUCASFILM'S
ALIEN
CHRONICLES™

THE CRIMSON CLAW

*Coming to bookstores
October 1998!*

FORTY-SEVEN DAYS OF spaceship travel, locked in a passenger cubicle since she was now too valuable to ride in a cargo pod, another seventeen days of quarantine to survive her inoculations and to pass customs, then a final transferal of deed and title on the shipping dock of a strange port city on a strange world called Fariance.

Ampris stood patiently in her restraint cables, ignoring the Bizsi Mo'ad handler who was finishing the last items of business with the Galard representative. Nothing they said or did was of interest to her. She stared at the odd sky overhead, noting that it was pale lavender with fluffy white clouds tinged a smoky blue shade underneath. Double suns hung low in the afternoon sky. They looked dim, small, and hazy. She did not like how they cast a double shadow. Everything seemed blurred around her, not quite real.

The air was cool and crisp, like autumn descending into winter. Ampris shivered lightly beneath her fur, missing the hot sunshine of Viisymel already.

A tap on her shoulder pulled her from her thoughts.

"Pay attention," the Viis from Galard Stables said to her. He spoke the abiru patois rapidly.

Ampris glanced around and saw that the handler from Bizsi Mo'ad was gone. Not caring, she backed her ears. The school was behind her now. She must look ahead and adapt herself to this newest life.

"You are called Ampris," the Viis said. He did not inflect it as a question, yet he waited as though expecting an answer.

"Yes," Ampris replied. She kept her voice low and submissive, because she wore a restraint collar. He carried the transmitter on his belt now, she noticed.

"What is your age?"

Impatience jabbed her. Hadn't he examined her paperwork? All her statistics should be on the invoice in his hands, but she knew better than to say so. This interrogation was a test of some kind. The Viis always loved to play games with their slaves.

Swallowing a sigh, Ampris said, "I am seventeen in Aaroun years, fully adult in weight and height. I am vi-adult in Viis—"

He pressed the transmitter, and her collar jolted a quick burst of energy to her vocal cords, silencing her.

"Don't do that again," he said.

Ampris bowed her head at once in submission, although inside she battled feelings of rebellion. Why was it wrong for any member of the abiru folk to display intelligence? Why was it so forbidden to make comparisons between abiru and Viis? It wasn't as though any of the abiru races had much in common with their Viis masters. The Viis controlled everyone and everything. Why, then, were the Viis always so touchy, so defensive?

Were they afraid?

With sudden insight, she flicked up her gaze to study the Viis male before her.

He was not as tall as most males, but he had the fashionable proportions and gracefulness of movement considered so pleasing in the Viis. His rill folds lay thick and luxuriant over a tall collar of engraved brass. His pebble-textured skin was shaded in attractive hues of gold, bronze, and green. Large, intelligent yellow eyes stared at Ampris now without betraying emotion, still evaluating her, still measuring her.

He did not look afraid. He looked assured and competent. Ampris told herself to forget her fanciful thoughts. This was no time to philosophize. She must pay attention.

He flicked out his tongue. "At Galard, you will do as you are told. You will be respectful of your superiors at all times. You will train hard. You will fight successfully. Those are your duties. If you complete them well, you will be rewarded well. If you are lazy, insolent, or cause trouble, you will be punished. If you lose repeatedly in competition, you will be sold. Is this understood?"

He spoke clearly, yet without disdain. There seemed to be no arrogance in him; he addressed her as a rational being, not as a slave kept only to do his bidding. Ampris found herself liking him, although she immediately crushed the feeling. Perhaps he was as decent as he seemed. Perhaps he would be a good master, but she did not know that yet.

"Yes," she answered. "I understand my duties."

"Good. You seem to be an intelligent Aaroun. That is in your favor. Are you willing to learn, Ampris?"

She backed her ears. "I know my drills—"

Seeing his eyes narrow, she stopped in mid-sentence.

Unsure how she had erred, she dared say nothing more. He stared at her in a silence that grew uncomfortable, and when next he spoke his tone was colder: "I have watched your training vids as well as your graduation combat at Bizsi Mo'ad. It was my suggestion to the school that you fight an instructor, and without the assistance of your conditioning modulator. You passed that test well enough."

Astonished, Ampris stared at him. Did he have that much influence? So much that he had only to make a request, and the school modified its combat evaluations to suit him?

But then, he did work with the famous Blues, the most successful gladiator team in the games.

"You show considerable promise," he said to her now. "But your training is only beginning. There is much still for you to learn."

Ampris met his eyes. "What I learn, I do not forget."

"Come then." He turned and lifted his hand in a wave. Ampris heard the engine of a transport start up in the distance.

Moments later, the craft rumbled up to them and halted, hovering above the ground. It was heavy and utilitarian, larger than the city transports she was used to seeing in Vir and Malraaket. Dark brown dust coated its undercarriage, partially obscuring the crest of its owner. She did not recognize the coat of arms and knew then that Lord Galard's estates and title were entirely colonial. He was not a member of the Twelve Houses. That meant his lineage would not be considered distinguished by Viisymel standards, and he would not be received at the imperial court. But with his obvious wealth, perhaps he did not care.

Ampris told herself she had no business judging her newest owner, whom she would probably never meet or see.

The Viis trainer now looked at Ampris again, as though weighing something. Then he said, "I am Halehl, chief trainer to Galard Stables."

Awed that she had been collected by someone so important, Ampris told herself she should have been more respectful. She bowed in silence.

He seemed pleased by her gesture of respect. "You have been trained in court manners, I see."

"Yes, Master Halehl."

"Very attractive. You were once the pet of the sri-Kaa, were you not?"

Ampris suddenly had to struggle to keep from snarling. "Yes."

"I thought so. Your provenance is muddled, but I recognized you from old newsvids. Well, pretty manners will not help you in the arena. You will have to be quick, well-trained, and savage. Is this understood?"

"Yes, Master Halehl."

He opened the cargo doors at the back of the transport. "Climb inside."

Ampris obeyed, her restraint cables making her clumsy, and Halehl shut the doors behind her. She heard the security bolts engage with swift thuds, and her heart sank. At last she was here, ready to begin her new life as a killer. Halehl's decency only seemed to make things worse.

As soon as he climbed aboard, he spoke a soft, quick command to the Gorlican driver, and the transport lurched forward.

They were slow to clear the dock traffic and congestion, but once they finally headed down the streets of this city, very little traffic could be seen.

The avenues were broad and free of pollution, lined with stately villas spaced well apart. Shops stood clustered in their own separate districts. Tall trees with spindly trunks and strange puffs of foliage at their tops swayed lightly in the cold breeze. The air smelled metallic and clean—very foreign to her nostrils. She found herself missing the heat of Viisymel's arid plains, the bright sunshine, the slow turgid rivers that smelled of reeds and fish.

The transport crossed one canal flowing straight, narrow, and green between a row of tall buildings, but Ampris saw no other water. Buildings spread farther apart as they reached the outskirts, then they were heading into rural countryside. For nearly an hour the transport flew past rolling meadows bordered by thickets of undergrowth and tall trees. Ampris found it strange that they met no other traffic on the road. Saw no dwellings, passed no village clusters. This was an empty world, Ampris thought. From her old lessons, she knew that not all the colony worlds were heavily populated. Sometimes, the Viis established only a central port, with a governor, a military station, and little else to hold their claim on a planet. Ampris wondered what the native folk of Fariance were like. She had seen none yet. Perhaps there were none on this dim, cold world with its muted colors and blurred double suns. Perhaps the Viis had long ago killed them all or deported them to work elsewhere in the empire.

To Ampris, this world seemed an unimportant place for the most popular gladiator stable to be based.

The twin suns were sinking to the horizon by the time the transport passed through gates that were paneled with tall iron spears. Carved beasts with snarling fangs and extended claws stood atop the gateposts. Then they were winding along a lane bordered on both sides by heavy woods. The ground rose in a long sloping hill, and halfway up the woods stopped. Ampris saw a villa stretching across the crest of the hill.

In the murky remnants of sunshine, the building stood gray, square, and solid—its architectural lines unfamiliar to her. Towers flanked it, and at the rear she glimpsed a tall, solid wall enclosing a compound of some kind.

At the front, the house was aproned by elaborate gardens of

low, clipped hedges planted in intricate patterns of knot and curlicue. Stone-paved walkways curled among the tiny hedges in pleasing patterns. But there were no flowers of any kind, no fragrance beyond that of tilled soil, shrubbery, and trees. Ampris sniffed, and found the garden a peculiar and unappealing vista.

The transport made its way around to the rear of the massive house—much larger up close than it had seemed from a distance—and lurched through a gate into an enclosed courtyard.

Once it parked on hover and Ampris was let out of the cargo hold, she stood quietly while her restraints were unlocked. Then she stretched fully, taking pleasure in unrestricted freedom of movement for the first time in too long.

From an upstairs window overlooking the courtyard, she saw movement and a glimmer of a face watching her. Then the watcher was gone, and Ampris wondered if she'd imagined it.

Halehl pointed at the upstairs windows rowed at regular intervals around the courtyard. "The fighters' quarters," he said. "Yours are at the end, over there." He pointed at a window, and Apris found herself suddenly astonished.

"No barracks?" she blurted out before she could stop herself.

Halehl flicked out his tongue, and overlooked her transgression. "You are a professional now," he said, sounding amused. "Ah, Ruar," he said to someone approaching from behind her. "Come and get Ampris settled. We'll start her training tomorrow, but let her adjust to the climate and gravity for the rest of today. Take her around the training grounds. Let her sniff and look all she wants."

Ruar proved to be an elderly Myal with silvered fur and extremely short, bowed legs. His mane was so sparse only a few strands floated around his face. His eyes were dark and rheumy, and he bowed to Halehl with a type of habitual anxiety not often seen in his kind.

"As the master says," he replied, bowing again. "And the evening meal?"

"No," Halehl said, puffing out his air sacs thoughtfully. "I think not just yet. Keep her isolated from the others. They'll meet her soon enough. I want to watch her train alone for a few days. Then we'll integrate her with the team."

Ruar glanced at Ampris as though she had just made his life harder. "They will want to see her," he objected, wringing his thin, bony hands. His prehensile tail was coiled tightly around one of his legs. "Master knows how Ylea is."

"Ylea will have to wait, just like the others," Halehl said firmly. "I don't want any turf fights. Is that understood? They will keep their distance until I allow the integration."

"As the master says," Ruar said with another bow.

Halehl flicked his fingers in dismissal, and Ruar gestured at Ampris.

"Come, come," he said.

She followed him beneath an arched overhang leading to a flight of stairs, but before they could climb them, a door slammed from above and footsteps came thudding down the stairs toward them.

An enormous female Aaroun, spotted in shades of brown and fawn, blocked their path. Garbed in loose, quilted trousers and a sleeveless vest, she was the biggest female Ampris had ever seen, with exaggerated muscle development that rippled beneath her glossy fur. Her neck and shoulders were massive, adding to the impression of sheer physical power. Despite that, her face was feminine, almost dainty, with long-lashed eyes tilted ever so slightly. Her ears were rounded and fringed with cream-colored fur on the tips. She flicked them back now, setting the ownership cartouche in her ear jingling.

Ampris noticed she wore much additional jewelry as well. Multiple necklaces hung around her neck. Rings glittered on every finger. Her claws were painted carmine, and she wore matching wrist cuffs of heavy gold.

Ampris could not help but stare at this creature. She had never seen a slave wear so much adornment before.

"Ruar," the Aaroun said in a silky, dangerous voice, "what kind of *ruvt* you bringing to our quarters?"

The word she spoke was an insult, very dirty. The fur bristled around Ampris's neck, and her lips curled back from her teeth.

Ruar glanced between them nervously, coiling and uncoiling

his long tail as he did so. "Now, Ylea," he said in a placating voice, "don't cause trouble. The master says to stay away from this one for a while. You know the rules."

Ylea gripped Ruar's scrawny shoulder with her red-tipped fingers and moved him aside. Then she stepped right up in Ampris's face and sniffed the air.

This additional insult was worse than the word she'd called Ampris. Angered, Ampris fought to keep still, to keep from snarling openly. But now the hair was standing erect along her spine. She narrowed her eyes to slits and growled a low warning in her throat.

"Stop it. Stop it," Ruar said in alarm. He fumbled for the transmitter at his belt and pushed it, sending a jolt into Ampris's throat.

She coughed and took an involuntary step back, furious with him for overreacting. This giantess wore a restraint collar too. Why wasn't he punishing *her*?

Ylea advanced on Ampris, crowding her again, giving her little pushes back into the courtyard. "You think you can just come here like a princess, one of us from day first? You think you so golden, so pretty, we like you? You think you any kind of match for our team? Hah! You half our size, puny *ruvt*. You like weed, get snapped in half, in first combat."

Ampris felt dwarfed by Ylea's muscular bulk, but also sized her up in seconds and realized she was slow, almost ponderous, in the way she moved. Ampris could run rings around this behemoth, but she wasn't ready to betray that yet.

"I've already drawn my first blood," Ampris said proudly, refusing to back up again. She stood with Ylea towering over her, and held her ground. "I haven't been snapped in half yet."

Ylea's tilted eyes closed to slits. "First blood?" she repeated, then roared out a laugh. "*First?* One combat and you dare speak to me? Be silent—"

As she spoke, she raked her claws at Ampris's face, but Ampris moved in swift reflex to grip Ylea's wrist and hold it.

Surprise darted through Ylea's eyes before her face contorted with fury. She bared her teeth, roaring a challenge, and yanked her wrist free.

Ruar darted up and stepped between them. "Ylea, stop it!"

Ylea slapped him aside, sending him tumbling to the pavement, and leaped at Ampris in a body tackle that took her down.

It was like being landed on by a boulder. Ylea's weight drove most of the air from Ampris's lungs. She grappled desperately, trying to keep Ylea's snapping jaws from her throat.

A fang grazed her shoulder, and Ylea's claws dug in like spikes. But when a whipcrack sounded overhead, Ylea jerked back with a snarl.

"Get up!" It was Halehl's voice, deep with anger. He cracked the whip across Ylea's broad shoulders a second time, cutting a gash in her vest. "Get up and form ranks. *Now!*"

Ylea scrambled to obey him, and quickly stood with her shoulders hunched and her eyes sullen.

With his rill crimson and at full extension behind his head, Halehl paced in a circle around Ylea. His eyes were blazing, and even his heavy tail was switching back and forth beneath the long skirt of his coat. Without warning, he lashed her with his whip a third time.

Ylea flinched but made no sound. One of her necklaces, broken by the lash, fell in a glittering heap at her feet.

"Stand there," he told her. "Do not move."

Ylea slitted her eyes and opened her mouth.

"Silence!" Halehl shouted.

Halehl turned to Ampris, who was still sprawled on the ground. "Get up."

She scrambled to her feet quickly, brushing dust off her coveralls, and felt both rumpled and humiliated. So much for being the bright new gladiator of the team, she thought.

"Did she bite you?" Halehl demanded.

Ampris shook her head.

He glared at her as though he blamed her for this, then snapped his head around at the old Myal limping over to them. "Ruar, you fool! I gave you strict orders not to let this happen."

"He tried to carry out your orders," Ampris said instantly in Ruar's defense.

If possible, Halehl's rill turned an even darker hue of crimson. "Hold your tongue, you impudent cub! Already you forget your orders. Already! Within a quarter hour of your arrival, you have disrupted and disobeyed. One more infraction, and it will be the whipping post for you."

Ampris dropped her gaze and said nothing more. Her eyes were burning, and she kept her jaws clamped tightly together.

"Ruar," Halehl said, turning on the Myal once again while the short male cringed visibly and coiled his tail around one leg, "get Ampris to her quarters *now*. See that she stays there."

"As the master says." The Myal snapped his bony fingers at Ampris and gestured urgently.

She stepped around Halehl and the glowering Ylea in immediate obedience. Ylea turned her head to follow Ampris's movements. Her lips skimmed back from her large, yellow teeth, and she growled.

Ampris hurried past her and followed Ruar up the stairs.

Behind her, although she dared not glance back, she heard Halehl's furious voice continue, although now his words were spoken too low for her to understand. She also heard the lash land again and again on Ylea.

Ampris sighed to herself. If she knew Ylea's type, Ylea would blame her for the punishment and hate her more than ever.

Ruar was limping along fast on his short, bowed legs. He shook his head. "Not good. Not good," he said. "Already you cause trouble."

"It wasn't my fault," Ampris said in annoyance. "Ylea started it."

"Your being here started it," Ruar insisted. "You."

Reaching a door at the end of the corridor, he unlocked it and flung it open. "Your quarters," he said. "You stay inside until I come back tomorrow."

"But—"

"Inside! Inside!" he said, almost frantically, glancing over his shoulder as though he expected Halehl to come after him next with the whip. "Now. There can be no more trouble today. Enough has been done already."

"She started it," Ampris said. It was important that he acknowledge the truth. She knew that trouble and blame could ripple out from this incident unfairly, keeping her from being accepted by anyone on the team. "I did nothing to her."

"You came here," Ruar said, refusing to meet her eyes. "That is enough for Ylea."

"Then she'll have to get over the problem."

Ruar sighed. "No," he said softly. "You will."

He pointed again at the door and Ampris stepped through it. But she paused on the threshold and turned back to him. "Is she the team leader?"

"Of course."

"Then how do I appeal to her good side?" Ampris asked. "I will not apologize, but how can I make friends with her?"

Ruar stared at her as though his eyes would pop from his skull. "Friends?" he squeaked at last. "Friends? There are no friends in the arena."

"But we're teammates, not competitors," Ampris said. "We're supposed to work together."

Ruar shook his head vehemently. "No friends. You stay quiet. Cause me no more trouble. Food will come soon, then you be very quiet."

"But, Ruar—"

He gave her a shove, hard enough to push her over the threshold, and swiftly slammed the door.

Annoyed, Ampris gave the door a kick, and in response the locks engaged.

She fumed a moment, glaring at the door, then recovered her temper and swung around to see her latest cell.

It was beautiful. It was spacious. It appeared to be filled with every luxury.

Astonished, Ampris forget all about her anger. At first, she could do nothing but stare. She kept thinking this had to be a mistake. She was a slave. She'd come here to be an expendable gladiator, useful until she made a fatal mistake or met her match in combat.

But to be given such a room . . . it reminded her almost of Israi's sumptuous apartments in the palace, and for a moment Ampris's eyes stung with tears of remembrance.

Dusk closed her window now with shadow, but a trio of lamps burned softly around the room. It was furnished as a sitting room, with hangings of lavender and mauve silk, soft chairs filled with cushions, a slightly worn but handsome rug, and an assortment of small tables, one of which supported a geometric sculpture of Igthia crystal.

Ampris drew in a breath of wonder and went to examine the sculpture more closely. As soon as she touched it, she discovered it to be fake, merely a reproduction, but still . . . to have artwork of her own . . . she wondered if she had stepped into a dream.

After the plain, unadorned, utilitarian barracks of Bizsi Mo'ad, this was divine.

Delight spread through her. Ampris grinned, then rushed to explore further.

She found a curtained doorway off to one side that contained a tiny bedchamber barely large enough to hold a bed—a real bed and not just a hard bunk—plus a side table with lamp and a vid control, a vid cabinet, and a chest with pegs and drawers for clothing.

Beyond the bedchamber, Ampris found an equally small bathing room, with a sunken pool fitted with hydroponic jets, a steam cabinet, a massage table that unfolded from the wall, and a washing sink of reproduction crystal surmounted by a mirror that activated to shimmering, reflective life at her approach. In the ceiling, a tiny window showed her the first twinkles of alien stars.

Overcome, Ampris sank to her knees beside the pool and pressed her palms against the smooth coldness of the floor. All this was hers and hers alone.

Never, not even when she was a privileged cub inside the Imperial Palace, had she enjoyed private quarters of her very own.

She could not believe it.

Oh, much of the magnificence in these quarters was surface only. But Ampris did not mind if the rugs were old or if the materials were synthetic. She had never believed she would live this way, especially after she was cast out of the palace.

And now, unexpectedly, so much was hers.

After the harshness at Bizsi Mo'ad, where there was no grace, no comfort, nothing civilized, it was like being given breath again. Hope bloomed inside her for the first time in a long, long while. She could not believe this gift, this kindness, this generosity of her new owner. And to think that she had struggled to remain at Bizsi Mo'ad, completely unaware of the better life awaiting her in Galard Stables.

"Oh, thank you," she whispered.

Then tears filled her eyes. Flinging herself facedown on the floor, she wept long and hard.

She wept until all her tears were gone, and she was left empty and somehow comforted. Yet still she lay there with her cheek pressed to the floor. The air grew chilly, but she did not care. Exhaustion pressed her bones into lead. She could not move, did not wish to move. Oh, if only she could stay in here, surrounded by this gift, for a year of days.

A soft tapping interrupted her thoughts.

Startled, she jerked up her head, then sat swiftly at the sight of a shadowy figure standing in the doorway. Who was this intruder whom she had not even heard enter?

"Pardon," said a soft voice with the unmistakable shrill singsong tones of a Kelth. A very ill-at-ease Kelth. "I brought your grub—uh—your dinner. When you want it served, you tell me."

Ampris tried to fluff up the tear-matted fur on her face. "Thank you."

"Yeah. I'll activate the heaters now. Should have been on already. The nights here get cold enough to freeze your—uh, really cold. I just got assigned to your quarters, so things aren't as ready as they should be. Don't worry, though. It won't take me long to get this place whipped into shape."

No lamp burned inside the bathing chamber. She could not see the Kelth clearly, yet something about him seemed familiar.

She rose to her feet, feeling embarrassed by having been caught lying on the floor. "My rooms were locked. How did you get in?"

The Kelth bowed in the shadows. "I'm your servant, see? The locks ain't much, more for your protection than—"

"Protection from whom?" Ampris demanded. "Ylea?"

The Kelth yipped softly in amusement. "Ylea could come through the wall if she decided to. She's built like a Mobile Forces Tanker."

"I've met her," Ampris said.

He yipped again. "Yeah, you did. And she sat on you. Got herself whipped for it. Got herself assigned extra laps in the morning. She don't like you much."

Ampris sighed. "I'll have to make peace—"

"Don't go crawling to her!" he said in alarm, handing out advice as though she'd asked for it. "That's no way to handle her."

As a servant, he was impertinent and far too familiar for his position, but at least he talked to her freely. Ampris tilted her head. "For some reason Ylea is threatened by me—"

He snorted rudely. "Threatened? By what? Her quarters are twice the size of yours. She's team leader. She gets the top rewards, most of which she strings around her fat neck."

Ampris thought about having apartments better even than these. She was too grateful for what she had to feel envious. "So why is she mad at me? Why does she hate me?"

"Ylea hates everybody. She's supposed to. She's a pro gladiator, see? No sweetness and good manners in her. That's why she's team leader. It takes fierceness to make it in this business."

Ampris snarled ferociously, and the Kelth jumped backward with a yelp.

Ampris laughed at him, enjoying her joke. She walked past him while he cringed back, staring at her through the shadows. Ampris could smell the faint aroma of meat coming from the sitting room. It was cooked in savory sauce with many spices, not all of which were recognizable. Her stomach rumbled, and her mouth filled with saliva.

The Kelth followed her at a safe distance, and Ampris laughed to herself again. No one had told her she would have a servant of her own. She felt unreal, almost free, except for the collar around her throat and the locks on the door.

It had been a long time since she'd last been served. She remembered when she took such luxuries for granted, believing her golden, magical life with Israi would go on forever. Now she was afraid to believe in anything good, because the good things always got taken away.

The sitting room glowed with lamplight, enchanted and beautiful with its treasures. A small round table had been pulled into the open center of the room. A serving place was laid, with an empty platter and forks carved of ival—a fragrant, dense wood impervious to liquid. Covered dishes stood around the platter, arranged in order of size. In a glance, Ampris took note of the arrangement's composition and was amazed by it. Everything, from the dish placement to the alignment of the forks to the glowing touch of a single orange-colored flower laid diagonally across the center of the platter, told a poetic story. Indeed, she was being treated like aristocracy.

The Kelth servant had also pulled up a low reclining couch for her to eat in the Viis manner.

Seeing it, much of Ampris's pleasure crashed down. She backed her ears. "Take that away," she ordered without glancing at the Kelth behind her. "I will eat like an Aaroun, upright."

"Sure," the Kelth said without apology. He scurried past her to shove the couch back in its original place.

As he selected a hassock instead and maneuvered it over to the table, the lamplight fell across his face and shoulders, illuminating him clearly for the first time.

He was leggy and tall for a Kelth, thinner than he should have been. When he straightened and turned around, something about the twitching of his pointed, upright ears, something about the shape of his slim muzzle, something in his quick, sidelong glance made him look like someone she should know.

Ampris stared at him, trying to grasp the memory without success. "What is your name?" she asked him.

He glanced at her again, with that familiar darting, sideways cast of his eyes. "Don't you remember me, Goldie? Don't you remember the auction? You've come a long ways since then, you have."

The old nickname clicked everything into place for her. Recognition flooded her, and she gasped. "Elrabin!"

His lips peeled back from his pointed teeth in a grin, and his eyes filled with a look of glinting mischief that she well recalled. "That's me," he said. "I didn't think you would remember me."

Delighted, she rushed to him, ignoring his cautious flinch back, and slapped him on both shoulders. "Of course I remember you. How good it is to see you. I did not think we would meet again."

"No," he said, glancing down shyly. "I didn't think so either."

"But how do you come to be here?" she asked him. "Tell me your story. I thought you were sold to the gladiators. You should have been in the ring—"

"I'd be dead by now, wouldn't I?" he said. "Gladiator bait's all I'm good for."

"Don't say that. You're quick and agile. You—"

"Look, Goldie," he said in a voice that stopped her. "I ain't got the knack for fighting. Never did. But I got a head for details, and my talents work fine at this. Serving. It's a relief to me, not to have my hide tacked on some gladiator's door like a trophy."

She didn't know what to say to that, so she smiled at him again. "I am so amazed that you are here, that we are here together. To see you again, after all this time—it's astonishing. I feel that Fate must have brought us back together."

Elrabin's ears twitched. Swiftly he clenched his fist, tapped it, and blew on it in a quick, superstitious motion that amused her. "Maybe it did."

She touched the Eye of Clarity hanging around her throat, wondering a little.

ABOUT THE AUTHORS

KEVIN J. ANDERSON and his wife, **REBECCA MOESTA**, have been involved in many STAR WARS projects. Together, they are writing the fourteen volumes of the Young Jedi Knights saga for young adults, as well as creating the Junior Jedi Knights series for younger readers. Rebecca Moesta also wrote the second trilogy of Junior Jedi Knights adventures (*Anakin's Quest*, *Vader's Fortress*, and *Kenobi's Blade*).

Kevin J. Anderson is the author of the STAR WARS: Jedi Academy Trilogy, the novel *Darksaber*, and numerous comic series for Dark Horse comics. He has written many other novels, including three based on *The X-Files* television show. He has edited three STAR WARS anthologies: *Tales from the Mos Eisley Cantina*, in which Rebecca Moesta has a story; *Tales from Jabba's Palace*; and *Tales of the Bounty Hunters*.

For more information about the authors, visit their Web site at

http://www.wordfire.com
or write to AnderZone,
the official Kevin J. Anderson Fan Club, at
P.O. Box 767
Monument, CO 80132-0767